OTHER BOOKS BY JESS MOWRY

For Dorrit Foxley

GHOST SHIP

JESS MOWRY

GHOST SHIP

ONE
En

D onte trudged wearily to the wagon and heaved the big
burlap sack off his shoulders. It thudded atop the others
he'd loaded and puffed out a pale cloud of dust. Each sack
weighed almost as much as himself; and he paused to wipe sweat
from his chubby-cheeked face, which was large onyx-eyed and pertly
snub-nosed above full lips always parted at rest revealing the gleam
of ferocious front teeth. Donte was thirteen and muscular, though
his muscles were padded with chubbiness in a cherubically charming
way, his chest a proud pair of oval shapes, his biceps roundly
prominent under skin of a dusky, sooty shade, though now striped
like a zebra with sweat and white dust. He wore only ragged cutoff
jeans that bared robust hips like a loincloth with pockets and seemed
to be more decoration than clothes, leaving a lot of his plump
bottom bare, while the roll of his belly spilled over in front, his navel
a funnel-shaped cave into night.

The evening sun was a blazing brass ball as it sank toward the
turquoise sea in the west; and Donte faced it, spreading his arms to
welcome a rising breeze on his body, while seabirds circled and soared overhead, calling down avian curses on him for still being there
when they wanted to land. But then, as if hearing a distant hail, he

1

turned to the east and studied the sky, which was cloudless and soft-ly shading to rose, and cocked his head as if listening. He remembered a seafaring proverb -- *Red sky at night, sailor's delight* -- yet he frowned for a moment.

The wagon, only a flat bed of planks mounted on four iron-spoked wheels from a 1917 Liberty truck, was hitched to an even older steam tractor that looked like a little locomotive fitted with Caterpillar tracks, and was parked on a small flat area at the rim of an ancient volcano. Specters of heat wavered up from its boiler like transparent phantoms entwining in dance, while a wraith of black smoke drifted out of its stack. Deep within the volcano's cone was a little lake that mirrored the sky, surrounded by vine-tangled trees. South-east, a hundred meters below, lay most of the tiny island; a patchwork of various well-tended crops interspersed with lush stands of green native forest.

Despite being tired from working since dawn, digging, sacking, and loading guano, Donte shook dust from his bushy hair and took a long moment to look around. He'd read many books about faraway lands, and seen many pictures in magazines, but Petite Orphelin Isle seemed a prettier place than anywhere else on earth.

Again he studied the eastern sky and seemed to listen for some-thing, but finally turned back to the west. Far out at sea was a passen-ger ship, probably bound for Jamaica. Closer, but still at considerable distance, a big motor-yacht was approaching, but would probably soon alter course... few foreign tourists visited Haiti, and none ever came to Little Orphan.

Down in the sea near the base of the mountain, a small open sloop with patched brown sails was expertly tacking through black lava reefs on a south-eastern course for the island's cove. Donte shaded his eyes with a hand and watched as the helmsman guided the boat through a foaming gap in the jagged rock teeth. To sail inshore was the fastest way home, but also a dangerous passage; and though Donte had often done the same, he would never have tried at this time of day on a wind shifting toward a lee shore. He watched until the boat cleared the rocks and reached deeper water in safety, then checked the tractor's water sight glass, adjusted a valve on the fuel-oil feed, then walked to a little three-sided tin shed.

Inside were piles of burlap sacks waiting to be filled, and an ancient machine to stitch them shut. There was also a wooden table and chair; and another boy lounged asleep in the chair with his bare feet on the table top. To say this boy was fat would have been an understatement of enormous proportions. Although the same age as Donte, sooty black and about the same height, he was over four times the diameter, his chest a pair of opulent orbs, his body mostly com-posed of rolls, his vast belly overflowing his lap; and though he was clad in cutoffs like Donte, little of them could be seen.

"Timothy," called Donte. "How many have we loaded this day?"

The fat boy opened his eyes, which were large, bright onyx, and usually cheerful in a face as round as an ebony moon, with cheeks overwhelming a wide, bridgeless nose. He yawned and stretched in a leisurely way, then carefully shifted his undulant mass in the very apprehensive chair and reached for a note pad on the table. "How many were loaded after our lunch?"

"*Ven,*" said Donte... Kreyol for twenty.

Timothy took a pencil and added numbers on the pad. "*Senkant,*" he said with satisfaction. "Fifty sacks we have loaded today while the men were at work on the schooner. Thanks to us she will have a full cargo."

"We make a good team, *mwen Chéf,*" said Donte.

"I am not your chief yet," said Timothy. "Our people will make that choice for themselves when my father retires."

"But for three-hundred years it has been the same choice and Little Orphan has always prospered."

"Thank you, loyal subject."

Donte came into the shade of the shack. A half-empty water jug stood on the table amongst the remains of a lavish lunch consisting of curried pork and rice, and he took it up with both hands, tilted it to his lips and gulped, then doused himself to wash off the dust.

"You must be tired," said Timothy.

Donte wiped gray mud from his chest. "Fifty sacks has been no fun, even with your companionship."

Timothy studied Donte. "But, what else is on your mind?"

Donte cocked his head. "Is my skull transparent?"

"Your face is sufficient barometer to show you have stormy thoughts."

Donte hesitated a moment. "...Andre dared the reef just now."

Timothy frowned. "On a shifting wind, and at low tide?"

"Perhaps there was a reason," said Donte. "Andre is not foolish. And with Thomas aboard."

Timothy considered. "Thomas may have been the reason. Still, I will speak to Andre. I will not have our fishing boat risked."

"Will you tell your father?" asked Donte. "Maybe I shouldn't have said anything."

"It was your duty to tell me, though my father need not know, and this is easily mended. ...Oh, and that reminds me; the stitching machine has jammed again."

"Easily mended," said Donte. From a goatskin pouch on the table, he selected a small monkey wrench and a wooden-handled screw-driver, which though ancient, were polished and oiled, and tinkered with the machine. Then he inserted an empty sack and revolved an iron wheel, watching a big needle jab and retract. "Good as new for the next century."

"You're as skilled with machines as your father."

"Which seems only natural, as is your diplomatic *forté.*"

Timothy avalanched out of the chair, all his rolls rearranging them-selves and his vast belly cascading down to his knees as he leaned far backward to balance its bulk, his tunnel-like navel aimed at the earth, his back swayed into a drastic curve, as Donte returned his tools to the pouch and slung it over a shoulder on its leather strap. Then the boys went out to the tractor, Timothy's body rippling all over with every ponderously waddling step.

The machine, though over a century old, was freshly painted silver-gray, its mechanisms, gears and controls all well greased and lubricated, its brass fittings brightly polished, including a plate on the boiler:

HORNSBY CHAIN TRACTOR
LINCOLNSHIRE, ENGLAND, 1904

With assistance from Donte, Timothy mounted one of the tracks to settle his voluminous bulk on a seat upholstered with goatskin. Donte followed him aboard, squeezing himself beside the huge boy as if melding into midnight softness, adjusted the fuel valve and gripped the controls, but paused and raised his head to face east in an alertly listening pose.

"You look like Anubis," said Timothy. "What do you hear?"

"...Nothing," said Donte after a moment. "I just have a feeling."

"Can you describe it?"

Donte searched the eastern horizon, darkening now as sunset neared, the placid sea shimmering reddish-gold, and not a ship or sail to be seen. "Only as if... *something*... is out there. ...And perhaps coming our way."

Timothy also scanned the sea, then raised his eyes to the cloudless sky. "It is too early for hurricanes, though they seem to come earlier every year, and with more ferocity."

"That is climate-change," said Donte. "And the ocean level is rising as the earth's polar caps melt."

"Fortunate then," said Timothy, "that we are a sea-faring people. We will listen to the weather report before the schooner sails."

Donte checked the pressure gauge, then gently opened the throttle. The tractor shuddered a moment like something coming to life, then piston rods began to thrust, a massive flywheel started to spin, and, chuffing and puffing, with jets of steam spurting and black smoke billowing out of the stack, it lumbered away with the sack-laden wagon, its iron tracks squealing and clanking on rock as it reached the volcano's rim and descended, chugging down a deeply-worn trail. The grade was steep as the trail snaked down toward the little lake in its green bowl of forest, and Donte eased the throttle in as the heavy wagon pushed them on. The air was cooler amongst the trees, but Donte was shiny and dripping sweat from pushing and pulling long heavy levers to steer the lurching and leaping machine. The trail leveled off to circle the lake, and Donte opened the throttle again, the tractor chuffing steadily as the wagon lumbered along behind. Tim-othy lounged back in the seat with his massive arms crossed behind his head, while the spheres of his chest quivered and quaked and his belly rippled like ocean waves to the rocking and jolts of the tractor, which clattered and clanked beneath towering trees leaving a specter of smoke in its wake. Sunlight shafted down through the leaves, golden now in late evening, and bright-colored birds flew squawking and screaming, disturbed by the noisy invasion. Donte opened the throttle wide as they emerged from the forest, and the tractor, spout-ing ebony smoke, clawed its way up to the top of the rim, balanced there for a breathless moment, then dropped its nose with a bone-shaking crash and descended toward the fringe of forest encircling the mountain's base. Donte battled the levers again as they tossed and pitched down the slope.

Timothy asked, "Is she under command?"

"She responds to the helm at least," puffed Donte, his chub-padded muscles showing themselves as he yanked and shoved the controls. "But I would not ask her to stop at the moment."

The trail veered south at the foot of the mountain, muddy and soft under centuried trees, and the rattling tracks threw mud everywhere. They lumbered past the village graveyard, with headstones painted in many hues that rivaled the flowers blooming amongst them. Timothy seemed to be napping, but asked without opening his eyes, "You are thinking of your mother?"

Donte looked back at the peaceful graveyard. "It has been two years, but I still miss her."

Timothy touched Donte's shoulder. "She will always live in your heart."

TWO
De

The tractor chuffed and clattered on through twilight's deepening shadows, but Donte knew the way by heart and ducked the occasional low-hanging vines that dangled like sinuous snakes from trees. Night birds started to twitter and chirp, and bats flitted silently past, some as big as foxes. The trail crossed a brook several times, the tractor splashing and flinging up spray that hissed and steamed on its boiler. A slim silver crescent of moon like a smile had materialized in the deep-purple sky as they finally rumbled into the village, which was only a score of small houses clustered beneath massive trees. The dwellings were various ages, the oldest of logs and ancient ship timber, the newer of plywood and packing crate planks; and all were raised on stones or blocks, roofed with rusty sheets of tin, their porches large and meant be used for sitting and reading and conversations. Their windows had screens instead of glass, with wooden shutters to close against storms.

Scents of cooking haunted the air like friendly welcoming spirits above the tractor's mechanical smells of fire, hot iron and oil smoke... rice and beans, fried plantains, and the rich aromas of goat meat and pork. The soft glow of candles and kerosene lamps glimmered from windows and open doorways, while children played hide-and-seek in the shadows or sailed model boats in the moon-sparkled brook that meandered its ferny-banked way to the cove. The younger children were naked; the older boys in cutoffs or shorts; while elder girls were dressed the same in addition to tank-tops or T-shirts. Many children were chubby and some were rolly-poly fat, though far from approach-ing Timothy's size; and even those of lesser mass boasted proudly prominent tummies carried on gracefully sway-backed builds; while brindle dogs with looping tails romped about with everyone. Donte nodded to Andre DeFoe, who puffed a slender cigar on his porch. He was fourteen, and the second fattest boy on the island next to Timothy, and reading *David Copperfield* by golden lantern light. Timothy signaled for Donte to stop, and asked, "How many fish today?"

"Four baskets," Andre replied, proudly puffing his chest.

"Very good work," said Timothy.

"In truth," said Andre, "Thomas pipes, and fish flock to the net."

"But you haul them in," said Timothy. "If you don't mind a suggestion, pack a larger lunch tomorrow so he won't ask you to do something risky to get him home for supper."

"But he is your brother."

"But you are captain at sea, and responsible for your vessel and crew."

Andre nodded. "*Wi, mewn Chéf.*"

"I'm not your chief yet," said Timothy. "But, even if so, I would bow to your judgment as captain at sea."

"I understand," said Andre, touching his forehead in salute.

Timothy nodded and Donte drove on. "That *was* easily mended," said Donte.

"We all have skills," said Timothy.

Younger kids ran to climb on the wagon for a short ride to the cove, Timothy's brother, Thomas, among them, though his goal was the tractor. He was eight and wondrously fat, his belly rolling upon plump thighs and plunging and bouncing with every bound, his cutoffs baring the moons of his bottom, while a wooden flute swung on a leather strip between the bobbing balloons of his chest. Donte stopped to boost him aboard, loading him onto Timothy's belly where he sank in as if on a pillow, then Donte resumed the controls.

"The schooner is almost ready," puffed Thomas. "The men are launching her now."

"*Bon,*" said Timothy, holding his little brother secure as he bobbed about on blubbery waves. "She can sail as soon as the cargo is loaded."

"The weather report," Donte reminded.

Thomas scanned the heavens. "The sky is perfectly clear."

"If you have a bad feeling..." said Timothy.

"Neither bad nor good," said Donte.

"But, that something is coming?"

"Or... maybe... waiting."

"Then we should consult Damon Millay."

"Supper is almost ready," said Thomas.

"Which reminds me," said Timothy. "That captains are in command at sea even if you are the Chief's son."

"...Oh," said Thomas.

They clattered away through a grove of palms to emerge on a white-sanded beach, where a forty-foot schooner was almost afloat, rolling on logs with a dozen men pushing.

"Everyone help!" ordered Timothy, and the children jumped to the ground and ran to add their shoulders, including Thomas at a rippling trot to put all his wobbly weight to use. The new copper sheets on the schooner's bottom gleamed in the glow of kerosene lanterns set here and there in the sand; and in minutes the vessel was floating free amid the cove's moon-sparkled wavelets.

Donte could never quite decide if Timothy's father, Jean-Luc Durant, reminded him more of a Sumo wrestler, or maybe a mighty model of Buddha. He wore only tan canvas shorts, which couldn't be seen in a full frontal view, and stood knee-deep in the shimmering water, talking with Donte's father, Paul, a handsomely muscular man.

"...three barrels of kerosene," Jean-Luc was saying. "And three of fuel-oil for the tractor, both of which are becoming expensive, so we must raise the price of guano another fifty *gourdes* per ton."

"I will inform the company, though I doubt if they will be pleased," said Paul.

Jean-Luc shrugged. "Men of business are seldom pleased to pay a fair price if they can pay less. Remind them that Cuba is not far away, and a company there has offered us more."

Paul touched his forehead. *"Wi, mwen Chéf."* He studied the schooner to see how she floated. "If we had a larger vessel we could trade with many islands."

"Perhaps one day," said Jean-Luc, and smiled at all the children. "Though they may be in charge by then."

"And the ocean may be bigger, and our island smaller." Paul glanced at a mountain of guano sacks on the beach nearby. "I will check for leaks while the crew goes to supper, then we will load her and sail at midnight."

Timothy called, "We should hear the weather report," while slowly unloading himself from the tractor.

"We have," said Paul. "Clear, with sufficient wind for good sailing."

Donte closed the fuel feed valve, let off the remaining steam with a WOOSH by opening another valve, then waded out to his father to get a hug, and a kiss on his cheek. "We should listen again before you sail. I feel there something out on the sea but I cannot define it."

"Then we will listen," said Paul. "Should we consult Damon?"

"She has said nothing?"

"*Non*, but, if you sense something amiss...?"

"If after supper I still have this feeling, I will ask her about it," said Donte.

Timothy waded out to Jean-Luc, his belly pushing a bow wave ahead, to also receive a hug and kiss. "Donte and I loaded fifty more sacks."

"An impressive day's work for two young men." Jean-Luc gave Donte a wink. "You must be tired."

"Hungry mostly," said Timothy.

"As am I," announced Thomas. "Four baskets of fish today."

"I am proud of you both," said Jean-Luc. "And no less of Donte and Andre."

Timothy asked, "May Donte have supper with us?"

"*Wi*, your mother already invited..."

The beach was suddenly lit bright as day as the blue-white beam of a powerful searchlight stabbed across the water. Jean-Luc shaded his eyes with a hand and peered toward the rocky jaws of the cove. "Now what is that? ...Not a gunboat, I hope. I thought those unpleasant times were over."

Donte's father faced the glare as the searchlight probed for a way through the reefs. "A gunboat would wait until morning. The last one to try our passage at night got stuck on the reef for three days and a tug was required to pull her off."

"I saw a motor-yacht," said Donte, "from up on the mountain a while ago, but I did not think she was coming here."

"She seems to be trying," said Jean-Luc. "Launch the longboat and guide her in. Hurry or there may be a wreck."

Timothy grabbed a lantern. "We will signal them to wait."

"I'm coming, too!" piped Thomas.

"Get the rifle," said Timothy. "In case they are smugglers or pirates."

"Or terrorists!" puffed Thomas, lumbering off to the village.

"Perhaps that was your feeling?" Timothy suggested. "Something was indeed out there and has come to Little Orphan."

"...Perhaps," said Donte.

A short time later, the gleaming white yacht, twice the size of the island's schooner, diesel engines murmuring, let go her anchor within the small cove like an iron fist through liquid crystal. Her portholes and windows blazed with light that sparkled the water all around and brought curious fish to the surface. Donte pulled the oars of the twenty-foot longboat and squinted up at the teakwood decks. "Electric lights are painful."

Timothy, filling the sternsheets, shaded his eyes with a hand. "People must get used to them."

"But probably seldom see the stars."

Thomas, in the bow, held the "rifle," a massive old Hotchkiss machine gun longer than he was tall. "*Blancs,*" he observed, as two white men somewhere in their forties, tanned and slenderly muscular, clad in immaculate boating shoes, white cotton trousers and polo shirts, came out on deck to check the anchor. "Do you think they could be terrorists?"

Donte studied the men: he hadn't seen many *blancs* in his life, and only in Port-au-Prince when crewing on the schooner. "They do not look like terrorists."

"How do terrorists look?" said Timothy. "According to my father, many wear suits and ties these days. ...Thomas, ready your rifle."

"Shall I aim it at them?"

"That would be rude."

Thomas cocked the heavy bolt and its ominous clack echoed over the water.

The men traded uncertain glances, then offered their hands palms out.

Timothy smiled. "The universal sign of peace: 'see, I do not have a rock in my hand.' ...I wonder if they speak French."

"I doubt they speak Kreyol," said Donte.

"*Bonsoir*," called Timothy, using the French pronunciation. "Welcome to Little Orphan."

"*Bonsoir*," answered one of the men, who had neatly-trimmed sandy-blond hair. He seemed surprised to hear Timothy's French, though his own when he spoke was deplorable. The "rifle" obviously made him nervous despite being aimed at the stars. "Thank you for chaperoning our float. We entreat to make sounds with your ancient head."

Timothy murmured in Kreyol, "I believe he is trying to say, take me to your leader."

Thomas giggled. "They do not look like Little Grays."

Timothy said in French to the men, "I am the chief's son."

"As am I," said Thomas, and impishly added, "Also a male heir to the ancient head."

Donte poked Thomas and whispered, "Be quiet and tend to the gun."

"...Er," said the blond man. "A solo of engine marches unwell. We are desiring..." He searched for words, "a mender of mechanisms afloat."

Donte said in Kreyol, "My father could look at their engine."

"As could you," replied Timothy. "Since your father must ready the schooner."

"I have my tools."

"But, supper!" protested Thomas.

Timothy spoke to the men in French again, "We were about to dine, and you are invited. We can take you ashore if you wish."

"...Er... Thank you." The blond man conferred in low tones with the other, whose equally well-cropped hair was brown; and though they possessed different features, they very much resembled each other in some subtle way Donte couldn't define. They spoke in English, he noted, debating whether to come with the boys or use their own boat. He heard the words, "primitive" and "offended," murmured by the blond man.

To which the brown-haired man replied, "I hope it isn't fried caterpillars!"

"Starchy stuff, I'd guess," said the blond man, "judging from their obesity. Probably beans and rice from all their foreign aid. It probably won't kill us; just don't drink the water." At last he addressed Timothy in his horrid approximation of French, "Allow us a voyage in our own canoe, thus to avoid the discommode of replacing us under the sea."

Timothy grinned, but politely replied, *"Comme tu veux."*

The men went aft to lower an outboard-powered skiff, and Donte's eyes were drawn to a doorway as a boy of around his age appeared. The boy was barefoot and wore only jeans, which looked very ragged and tightly outgrown for someone aboard so splendid a vessel -- one knee ripped, and their cuffs dragging ribbons while straining skin-tight on his thighs and leaving his bottom half bare -- and though not far above Donte's weight, was very soft and wobbly fat like a boy made of cocoanut pudding, his chest a pair of melon-like shapes that bobbled and quivered with every movement, an undulant torus encircling his waist, chubby rolls squeezed under his arms, and his belly like a pendulous pillow hanging almost halfway to his knees, his navel tunneling upward and well below the reach of his hands. His face was pear-shaped, plump-cheeked and pug-nosed like those of newsboys in old-time cartoons, with fierce front teeth likely always displayed behind full lips at rest in a pout, while his shaggy mane of golden-blond hair tumbled in tangles over his shoulders and almost completely covered blue eyes. Compared to the men he was *very* white, his inverted nipples so pale a pink as to be almost unseen. A cigarette dangled from his mouth, and a green bottle by its neck in one hand.

It seemed odd to Donte that, while most of Little Orphan's youth were chubby or fat to some degree, and certainly none were skinny or frail, he was intrigued by this boy... perhaps because of his opulent softness, or maybe just because he was white in the seemingly whitest way possible.

Thomas remarked in Kreyol, "What a marvelous belly he swings! It rivals even yours, Timothy."

"A marvelous *shape*," agreed Timothy. "And remarkable for how low it descends, especially for a boy who doesn't weigh much more than Donte. ...Of course," he added, patting his own, "nowhere near the mass of mine."

"What is that bottle?" asked Thomas.

"Heineken," said Timothy. "A very expensive beer from Holland."

"Does it taste better than our beer?"

"That I doubt," said Donte. He compared the clothes of the men and boy. "One might think him the blond man's son, but why dress a rich boy so poorly?"

"Perhaps he is a crewman?" said Thomas.

"Observe his hands," said Timothy. "He pulls no lines, nor manually labors."

"A cabin-boy?" Thomas suggested.

"Or the cook, and if so a good one."

"That seems evident," said Thomas, "with such a wondrous apron of fat."

"But do not stare, it's rude," said Donte, while trying not to do so himself.

Aft, the men had their skiff in the water. The blond one noticed the boy and frowned. "I assume you'll be staying on board," he stated rather than asked in English.

The boy looked indifferent and started to shrug, but saw the longboat and came to the rail, his "newsboy" face lighting with interest, the orbs of his chest rolling over, and his pendulous pillow of belly protruding cheekily out beneath, its underside even whiter than the rest of him. "Woah, dude! You're awesome!" he exclaimed, obviously meaning Timothy.

"Randy!" yelled the blond man. "Shut up before you offend them!"

The other man muttered, "Lucky they can't speak English."

Timothy smiled at the boy and said in flawless English, "I am not in the least offended, and you are also awesome, dude. Will you come and dine with us?"

Thomas added, also in English, "Shoes and shirts are not required."

"I like the sound of that," said the boy.

THREE
Twa

Jean-Luc stood majestically on his porch as Donte, Thomas and Timothy escorted the visitors up from the beach, Donte toting the huge gun casually over a shoulder, and Thomas piping a cheerful tune in rhythm to their steps. The blond boy shambled along with them in a backward-leaning gait, puffing like the Hornsby tractor, his sagging jeans baring the moons of his bottom, as pale as the friendly smile in the sky, while the spheres of his chest jiggled and jounced and his belly quivered, shimmied and swung as if in joyful accompani-ment to the rippling earthquakes of two of his hosts.

The duo of men followed the boys, who had come ashore in the longboat powered by Donte's oarsmanship while they had motored behind. They were looking uncertain again, though the gathered villagers smiled at them and chided their children not to stare. Most of the older population had seen white men before, and the kids were charmed by Randy, especially his wondrous belly, which drew admir-ing remarks. The dogs were not as politely restrained, capering close to sniff at the guests while amicably wagging their loops of tails. Donte would have expected the men to stay instinctively close together in what was obviously to them a new and uncertain situation, but they kept a careful distance apart as if they'd had an argument.

Jean-Luc's front room was partly an office, lit by a kerosene lamp overhead, with an ancient desk and file cabinet. One whole wall was devoted to books. On another wall hung a map of the world, a pic-ture of Haiti's president, and an age-yellowed government paper granting Little Orphan's chief the power to execute people. Jean-Luc, in English, described his duties as he ushered the visitors into the kitchen, Timothy trailing close behind and Thomas eagerly after. Donte un-shouldered the gun, ejected the bullet, put it back in the drum, and stood the weapon by the front door, also un-slinging and leaving his tools.

"...Settle disputes," Jean-Luc was saying as Donte came into the kitchen. "Not that we have very many. Preside at weddings performed by our *Mambo*, fill out birth and death certificates, send copies to Port-au-Prince once a year. And keep records of our business, which is exporting guano aboard our schooner."

The blond man asked, "Don't you have a computer?"

"No need to digitize simple tasks when pen and paper suffice. ...Gentlemen, please be seated. ...And, as you may have observed, we are not possessed of electricity, having no fossil-fuel resources, nor the wealth to purchase enough to power a generator."

"You could use solar panels," the blond man suggested, taking a chair at an impressive table laid with white linen, fine china and silver. Candles burned in polished stands, and a powerful lamp with a porcelain shade cast a golden glow from a rafter. Thomas and Timothy seated themselves and motioned for Randy and Donte to join them.

"Or a wind generator," said the brown-haired man, taking a chair beside the other, though shifting it slightly away.

Jean-Luc smiled. "Enabling us to have televisions, video games and microwave ovens? ...Yes, we are aware of these things; the Internet and wireless phones, electric toothbrushes and can-openers. And all the other electronic charms... or, as some say, 'necessities'... of the so-called civilized world. Of course anyone may leave this island if they wish to seek them."

"Swim?" said the brown-haired man -- at least, thought Donte, partly in jest -- though drawing a warning look from the other.

Jean-Luc, still on his feet, laughed. "Our schooner sails monthly to Port-au-Prince; fishing vessels and cargo craft put into our cove for supplies or repairs; and anyone may build a boat if they wish to sail away."

"*Do* people leave?" asked the blond man, shifting his chair away from the other by a few centimeters. "I'd think your kids would be enticed..." He made a vague wave toward the ocean, "by all the modern things out there."

"I noted you observing the paper in my office. I assume you read French?" said Jean-Luc.

"A little better than I speak it. I spent a summer in Paris during my college days."

"In three-hundred years," said Jean-Luc, "no chief of this island has used that power to take the life of anyone. Banishment from Little Orphan is our harshest punishment, and that has only happened once... a hundred years ago."

"...I guess that means people are happy here," said the brown-haired man, also slightly shifting his chair to further distance himself from the other... making Donte wonder again if they'd had an argument. "But you don't... discourage people from leaving?"

Jean-Luc laughed. "We are not Luddites, but merely a small community of people who know when enough is sufficient."

The blond man glanced at Timothy, as if thinking his size much more than sufficient, but carefully asked, "Hasn't there been a lot of violence? ...I mean in Haiti's past."

"Sadly, yes," said Jean-Luc. "But not on Little Orphan. We are a part of Haiti, even though quite distant, as you no doubt observed on your chart, because of a choice made long ago when the Caribbean was being colonized by Europeans. ...Perhaps you would like to hear our story, but, of course, as we dine?"

"Of course," said the blond man politely.

"*Finally* we dine!" Thomas whispered in Kreyol.

Jean-Luc bowed. "Gentlemen, my wife, Angelique."

Everyone rose as a woman, as marvelously immense as her mate, and clad in her best gingham dress, appeared. "Welcome," she greeted the guests in English. "I apologize for the simple fare and regret I could not anticipate the pleasure of visitors tonight."

"It smells delicious," the blond man said... a fact no one with a nose would dispute.

Thomas grinned impishly. "The fried caterpillars especially."

"Thomas!" exclaimed Angelique, looking horrified.

Timothy smiled at the men, who looked a little discomfited. "Being a taste that must be acquired, we of course understand if you decline." He glanced at the wood-burning range. "But, there are other primitive dishes that civilized systems may survive, such as fried fish and roast chicken; the former... as may not surprise you... served on a bed of rice, though possibly redeeming itself with a garnish of citrus and peppers. The chicken attempts to please by the grace of its basting in wine sauce; and there is curried kid... of the quadruped kind, I assure you... along with... predictably... beans, though grown here on our island and not a gratuitous import. For the rest, there are only plantains, fruit, and a loaf of freshly-baked bread, with a humble desert of berry tarts. I fear we can only offer French wine, perhaps a passable *Pinot Noir*, as an hygienic alternative to our venomous water."

"Timothy!" exclaimed Angelique and quickly turned to the men. "I apologize for my sons. They are not normally rude."

The blond man looked sheepish. "The apology is on our side. We made a few... uniformed, remarks before we knew your... young men... spoke English."

"That is perhaps understandable," said Jean-Luc, while seating himself in a very substantial chair. "And boys will be boys."

The blond man looked relieved, though flicked a warning eye at Randy. "Yes, they will."

"My sons," said Jean-Luc. "Timothy and Thomas. And this is Donte Manuxet."

"I'm Jason Lancaster," The blond man said. "This is my friend, Walter Marsh. ...And my nephew, Randy. We're from America."

"North, South, or Central?" asked Timothy.

"...Er," said Jason. "The United States."

"Thomas," said Angelique. "Will you please pour the wine? ...And without impish comment."

Thomas avalanched to his feet and poured the wine into long-stemmed glasses. The "primitive fare," Donte noted, did seem pleasing to civilized palates; and Randy dug eagerly into his fish after taking a gulp of wine. "This rocks!" he proclaimed around a mouthful.

"He means it's very good," said Jason.

Jean-Luc smiled. "Thank you for the translation, though its meaning seems quite complimentary in its colloquial form."

Angelique beamed at Randy. "Thank you."

"You mentioned the history of your island," said Jason, after sampling his fish and obviously finding it worthy to rock.

Jean-Luc took a sip of wine. "We of course teach history to our children, and not exclusively, if you will pardon, the European version. ...Donte? If you wouldn't mind?"

Donte, after offering Randy the curried kid on a platter, and Randy massively piling his plate, took a sip from his wine glass and faced the two white men. "Of course you know of Christopher Columbus, who is credited with discovering your country in 1492... though it was actually Cuba. The Scandinavian Vikings, most notably Leif Erikson, had landed on your continent five-hundred years before; and there is also evidence of even earlier African voyagers..."

Jean-Luc chuckled. "You may advance a little in time."

Timothy laughed, having finished his fish, as had Thomas and Randy, and starting on the chicken. "He will soon have us back on Pangea!"

"...Well," said Donte, finishing his fish and refilling Randy's glass. "Returning to 1492, December fifth to be exact, Columbus discovered a large island... he had thought Cuba to be China... and named it Española, though it already had a name, and, of course, claimed it for Spain, regardless that people were already there and quite content to belong to themselves."

Jean-Luc prompted, "Perhaps still a little more recent."

"Hmm," said Donte, offering the chicken to Randy, who, though obviously listening, had been eating like a castaway rescued from starvation. "By the late 1600s, France had possession of Haiti... roughly a third of Española... along with other Caribbean isles, while England and Spain had taken the rest; and all had established economies dependent upon the labor of slaves."

"And you know where they came from," said Thomas, also busily eating.

Donte poked him and continued, "Thus far, this island had not been discovered by the Europeans, probably due to being so small. A slave ship... we know not of what country... was wrecked on the reefs in a storm. Her crew escaped in their boats, leaving their human cargo chained in the flooding holds to drown."

The white men were looking uneasy again, though Randy was listening intently while shoveling food and quaffing wine.

"Many did drown," Donte continued, offering Randy fried plantains. "Men, women and children. But some escaped as the ship broke up, and managed to swim ashore. Thus, our community was founded; and since we were orphans of Africa, we named our new home appropriately, though *Ketewa Agyanka* in our mother tongue. We assume the ship's crew perished at sea, since one of their capsized longboat... in which we guided you tonight... washed up on the beach a day after the wreck; and for almost a century there was no contact with Europeans."

He stopped for another sip of wine, and to refill Randy's glass. "But, as their presence multiplied in the Caribbean, we were at last discovered; first by the Spanish of Cuba, then by the English of Jamaica, both of whom wanted to claim us as their property."

He paused to accept a tart from Thomas and pass the tray to Randy, who served himself with three. "By then, in 1793, there had been a slave revolt in Haiti... the only successful slave revolt in all of recorded history... so it seemed prudent to become Haitian, though being so small and distant, we have seldom been involved in Haiti's turbulent affairs."

"Obviously not," said Jason, who was obviously enjoying his meal and finding the wine to his liking. "From what I've heard of Haiti, it's a very poor and hungry place, and..." He glanced at Timothy, "judging by what I saw of your people, you don't have those problems here."

"We enjoy the rewards of our labors, as all people rightfully should," said Jean-Luc.

Walter, perhaps emboldened by wine, said, "Maybe a little too much. Obesity..." He glanced at Randy, who was polishing off the last of his tarts, "especially in kids, is becoming a problem all over the world."

Jason, perhaps also emboldened, indicated the table. "And you seem to have so much. Doesn't that make you feel..."

"Guilty?" suggested Jean-Luc.

Both guests seemed to realize they might have made a *faux pas*, but Jean-Luc smiled.

"You have heard the admonition of parents to 'eat everything on your plate because children in other countries are starving?'"

"My mother used to say that," said Jason.

Timothy said, "But, it makes absolutely no sense, because, unfortunately, they will starve whether or not the child cleans his plate."

"At best," said Donte, finishing his tart, and again refilling Randy's glass, "it may make a child feel grateful to his parents and god for his own good fortune."

"And at worst," said Angelique. "It may make him feel guilty for having abundance while others must live in want."

"...Well..." said Jason carefully, "that's what I was saying, though not very diplomatically."

"I understand," said Angelique. "But, guilt is a crippling emotion to inflict upon a child. It is a form of punishment that damages more than enlightens. A child resents being made to feel guilty, and often transfers that resentment onto whatever he or she is forced to feel guilty about. ...To cite the example at hand, a child may begin to resent the poor, because the poor make them feel guilty."

Timothy added, "Do I help the hungry by cleaning my plate? If so, I certainly must. But, should I feel guilty for doing so because it doesn't actually help?"

Thomas patted his belly. "Does being fat prove that I help the poor? Or does it suggest I do not?"

"That's kind of... childish thinking," said Jason.

"Though logical," said Jean-Luc, "to the mind of a child. And perhaps an example of how the more fortunate in this world, even perhaps with the best of intentions, instill resentment of the poor in their young at early ages." He sipped the last of his wine and regarded his ebony vastness. "Should we then suffer ourselves to stay thin?

Deny ourselves what we have rightfully earned and go hungry to show our concern of the hungry, despite knowing that will not help them? ...Or, as 'civilized' people do, should we *waste* our abundance with needless exertion... 'work it off in a gym,' as they say... allowing us to consume it while deluding ourselves we are 'good' because we do not *display* our consumption? And, should we batter the minds of our children to conform their bodies to dictated shapes of a one-size-must-fit-all limitation... as even now being mandated in some 'enlightened' societies... and ridicule, shame, and humiliate them for what is per-fectly normal in nature... certainly not a 'disease'... to cripple them also with guilt?"

"...Well... of course that wouldn't help," said Jason.

"No, it does not," said Jean-Luc. "It merely instills another resent-ment: since it is 'good' to be thin, and one must suffer to not become fat, then those who are fat must be bad because they do not suffer, and therefore must be made to suffer."

"And while the thin are hating the fat the hungry still go hungry," said Donte.

Jean-Luc added, "We yearly ship part of our harvests to a child-ren's refuge in Port-au-Prince, not because we feel guilty, but because it is right."

"But, aren't you concerned about health?" asked Walter, flicking a guarded frown at Randy, who'd downed the last of his wine and blissfully sprawled back in his chair while unabashedly stroking his belly and politely half-muting a burp.

"The average life-expectancy of a Haitian male is forty-five years, a female forty-eight," said Jean-Luc. "My father... as ample as I... passed at the age of ninety-seven while fishing in the cove. And most of our families have living grandparents and great-grandparents of octogen-arian, nonagenarian, and even centenarian ages."

"You seem to eat healthy food," said Walter. "Organically grown, I suppose." He glanced again at Randy, who'd accepted the last of the tarts from Donte and, though seemingly with effort, was adding it to his cargo hold. "Not a lot of processed junk and empty calories like most American kids eat."

"And I assume you work hard," added Jason. "So you get lots of exercise."

Donte laughed. "Some of us more than others, though everyone doing what they do best benefits us all."

"We have a small gym on our boat," said Walter, with another glance at Randy. "At least Jason and I make use of it. I guess that's 'needless exertion,' but you don't get much exercise at sea."

"If you are powered by engines," said Thomas.

"...Er, speaking of which..." said Jason.

"One 'marches unwell,'" said Timothy.

"Donte?" said Jean-Luc.

"I will get my tools."

Jason and Walter exchanged glances, noted by Jean-Luc, who said, "I assure you that, next to his father, who is occupied loading our schooner, there is no one on Little Orphan as skilled with machines as Donte."

"We will row out," said Timothy. "Thus saving you the discommode of replacing him on the shore."

Donte turned to Randy. "Will you come with us?"

"Yeah," sighed Randy, swallowing the last bite of tart and muting another burp.

"I'm coming, too," said Thomas.

FOUR
Kat

"**M**an, I'm totally stuffed!" sighed Randy, pleasurably patting his pendulous belly as, swaying a little on his feet, he followed Thomas and Timothy into the house's front room.

Timothy smiled. "Your appetite compliments our cuisine."

Donte, trailing the other boys, gripped Randy's shoulders to steady him as he veered a bit to starboard.

"Guess I'm a little buzzed, too," laughed Randy, leaning on Donte for support; Donte's arm going around the roll where a slimmer boy's waist would have been, and finding Randy as supple and soft as he'd imagined he might be.

"That is our savage plan," said Thomas. "To fatten you further and douse you with drink so we may eat you tomorrow."

"Boiled in a big black pot," said Donte. "While we insert bones through our noses and dance."

Randy laughed. "Like in cartoons."

"Though you have such a marvelous belly," said Thomas, "which hardly needs further enhancement."

Again Randy patted himself. "Guess it is kinda cool." He smiled at Donte. "An' it just got a lot of enhancin'."

"You ate more than me," said Thomas. "Which is an accomplishment."

"And almost as much as me," said Timothy. "Which is a major accomplishment."

Randy laughed. "I don't wanna brag, but you should see me when I'm really hungry."

Then the boys fell silent as Jason and Walter came in from the kitchen along with Jean-Luc. Jason shot Randy a look of annoyance. "Pull up your pants. ...Are you all right?"

Randy didn't uplift his attire. "I feel a lot better than I have in a week."

Walter muttered, "Because you've gotten off your butt for the first time in a week."

Jason flicked Walter a frown, but said, "We're going back to the boat."

Jean-Luc bid the men *bon voyage* and bowed them out the door, then he turned to Randy. "*Are* you all right?"

"Sure," said Randy. "An' thank you for the awesome dinner, an' your wife, too."

"The pleasure was ours," said Jean-Luc, then returned to the kitchen to help Angelique with the dishes.

Timothy studied Randy, who'd draped an arm over Donte's shoulders for continued support, while Donte's arm still encircled his waist.

"Are you truly all right?" asked Timothy.

"Like I said, better than I felt in a week."

"Would you like a beer?" asked Thomas.

"You dudes got beer, too?"

"But of course," said Thomas, and padded into the kitchen. He returned a few moments later bearing an amber quartet of old-fashioned cork-stoppered bottles. Undoing the wire and pulling a cork, he offered one to Randy, who tilted it to his lips.

"This rocks!" Randy proclaimed, after transforming a tentative sip into a tremendous gulp.

"Is it better than Heineken?" asked Thomas.

"Way!" said Randy, and gulped again, his belly plunging and rebounding as if being depth-charged. "Kinda like kickin' creme soda."

Timothy took a bottle from Thomas. "It is our Little Orphan brew. Part of its intrigue is sugar cane."

"Man, if you sold this in Malibu you wouldn't have to sell guano!" said Randy, after a blatant burp. "...What is guano, anyway?"

"Old bird shit," said Timothy. "Accumulated for centuries atop our island's mountain. A fine organic fertilizer, and quite valuable."

"Malibu?" said Donte, as Thomas gave him a bottle. "The coastal city in California noted for its beach and surfing? Is that where you are from?"

A shadow seemed to cross Randy's face, and what could be seen of his eyes seemed to sadden beneath his golden mane. "Till about a year ago. ...Mom an' dad were killed in a car wreck."

"We are sorry," said Donte.

"Yes," said Timothy, touching Randy's arm.

"Truly," added Thomas, also with a touch. "But, did you surf?"

"Nah," said Randy. "Which is kinda funny, I guess, since we lived in a beach house." He paused to gulp more beer, then burped again and wiped his mouth. "My dad was kinda rich... had a software company that made a lot of cool games. His will left everything to me, but made Uncle Jason my guardian till I turn eighteen. Jason an' Walter live in Miami; that's where we started this trip. They're goin' to Jamaica for..." He seemed to consider, then finished, "their second honey-moon. ...They're gay, but they didn't want you to know."

"Ah," said Donte. "That would explain their staying unnaturally apart."

"As I also observed," said Timothy.

"And I," said Thomas.

"They were scared you might hate gay people," said Randy. "Like in some African countries. I heard 'em talkin' about it after one of the engines quit an' they saw your island. ...Um, do you?"

Timothy shrugged. "We never had any on Little Orphan; at least none noted in our history... though perhaps they did nothing notable. But, people should not be hated because of who they love. ...May I ask...?"

"I used to think I was bi," said Randy. "But I was into Emo stuff, an' my dad said it might be a phase. Believe it or not, I had a girlfriend back in Malibu."

"Why would we not believe it?" asked Donte.

"You are quite handsome," said Thomas.

"Thanks," said Randy, and laughed. "Walter says I look like an obese girl." He patted his chest. "Probably for obvious reasons."

27

Thomas patted his own chest. "We also have boy-breasts, as you may have noticed."

"And mine are quite impressive," said Timothy, "if I say so myself."

"As often you do," said Donte.

"You're both awesome," said Randy.

"Is it like having two fathers?" asked Thomas. "Living with your uncle and Walter? Even if they cannot replace your real father sadly lost."

Randy's expression hardened a little. "We don't have much in common." He took another gulp of beer. "An' not just 'cause they're gay. Like you might of noticed, they're into 'healthy' stuff. 'Specially Walter, who rags on me 'cause I won't 'get in shape.'"

Timothy frowned. "No one has the right to dictate the shape of another."

Donte smiled. "We like your present shape." Then he asked, "One of your engines malfunctioned? Both were running when you drop-ped anchor."

"It started again but it didn't run right... didn't have much power, Jason said. That's when he decided to come to your island."

Timothy went to a shelf, on which sat a black plastic radio about the size of a shoe-box. He wound a crank handle and clicked a knob, and a voice in English spoke of the weather.

"That's cool," said Randy. "No batteries."

"They are made in Africa; and for just that reason," said Donte.

Thomas added, "That is shortwave. It also receives AM and FM, so we hear news of the world, and rock."

"Don't you listen to rap?"

"Much of it sounds depressing," said Donte. "With so much rage against what is wrong, but so little hope to make anything right that it seems to only exploit what is wrong."

"Rollin' wit' mah bitches," said Thomas, striking a cartoonish threatening pose. "Bein' a bling-swaggin' thugger an' sippin' on gin an' joose. Cappin' niggas an' schemin' green 'cause I got it so hard in da 'hood."

Timothy switched off the radio. "Still predicting clear skies to-

28

night, with winds of five to fifteen knots."

"Slow, but steady sailing," said Donte. He turned to a barometer mounted on a wall. "It is falling a little."

"Do you still have a feeling?" asked Thomas.

Donte cocked his head as if to listen. "It seemed to disperse during supper, though then my mind was occupied." He faced the moon-sparkled ocean shimmering beyond a window. "But, still I feel as if... *something*... is out there."

"What you mean?" asked Randy. "Like... wait, I know the word... premonition?"

"*Wi*... yes," said Donte. "A feeling that something is coming from somewhere out at sea."

"Then," said Timothy, "we should consult Damon before the schooner sails." He drank the rest of his beer and opened the door to view the cove. "The last of the sacks are being loaded."

"Who's Damon?" asked Randy, after draining his bottle. "Like, your weather-person?"

"Our *Mambo*," said Donte, downing his beer. "Which is Kreyol for a priestess of *Voodou*."

"You dudes believe in Voodoo?"

"But of course," said Timothy. "Though we do not stick pins into dolls, as seems so widely believed by the world. Nor cast curses upon each other, or call up rotting *zonbis* from graves."

"Nor do *zonbis* eat brains," added Thomas, also finishing his beer.

Donte nodded. "*Voodou* is a good religion that teaches us to celebrate life and live in peace with all things, alive as well as spiritual. The word itself translates as spirit in our mother African tongue."

"You believe in ghosts?" asked Randy.

"They are another form of life beyond the physical."

"Can Damon tell fortunes?"

"She can often explain premonitions," said Donte, "such as this feeling that haunts me tonight. ...Would you like to come and meet her? Then we will look at your engine."

"Sure."

"I will carry your tools," said Thomas. He slung Donte's pouch over a shoulder and trailed his brother out the door.

"Woah!" said Randy, stumbling as he tried to follow. "Is there Voodoo in your beer?"

Donte smiled, still steadying Randy. "There is *Voodou* in everything; and the world might be a happier place if people honored it. ...Keep your arm over my shoulders."

"Hope it ain't very far," said Randy, as Donte guided him out on the porch. "Ain't done much walkin' this year."

"*Non*, not far," said Donte, helping Randy descend the steps, where a dozen dogs surrounded them.

"Those all yours?" asked Randy, rpeaching to pet furry heads.

"They are everyone's," said Timothy.

Thomas added, "It takes a whole village to raise a cub."

"I used to have a dog," said Randy. "But Uncle Jason's allergic so I had to give him away."

FIVE
Senk

The little village was quiet now beneath the tree shadows and silver moon-smile. Night birds called from the forest as gentle wavelets lapped on the beach; a soft breeze whispered though branches and leaves, and the faint voices of men at work carried from the schooner, while distantly from out in the cove came the low drone of the yacht's generator. Golden candle and lamp light shone from most of the dwellings' windows; and there was a glimpse as the boys passed a house of two young children naked in bed and their mother reading to them.

Randy sighed, an arm still over Donte's shoulders, and Donte's arm still around him as he shambled along. "My mom used to read me stories: *The Wind In The Willows* an' that kinda stuff."

"As did mine," said Donte. "She passed some two years ago. A tree fell during a hurricane."

"Sorry, man," said Randy.

Timothy and Thomas leading, and escorted by the dogs, they crossed a plank foot-bridge over the brook. Randy was evidently un-used to the steamy Caribbean heat, soon becoming shiny with sweat and glistening pale in the moonlight as if Donte was guiding a wan-dering spirit; though his scent was boyishly earthy and also hinted of certain exertions not needless -- as Donte had found last year -- performed on the physical plane.

"The fuck is *that?*" Randy yelped, pressing to Donte as something swooped past on leathery wings.

"A flying fox," said Donte. "They will not bite unless provoked."

"...Oh. Sorry."

Donte laughed. "We use that word when appropriate. It is very expressive in any language."

Thomas giggled. "Though my mother would wash out my mouth with soap if she heard me express it."

"You dudes sure speak good English," puffed Randy, pausing to wipe sweat from his face.

"Though somewhat archaic," said Timothy. "Judging from the vernacular we hear on radio. Damon teaches English and French, but most of our books are very old."

"Guess you read a lot."

"In lieu of television, the Internet and video games."

The largest home in the village wasn't Jean-Luc's, but Damon Millay's, and was also the schoolroom and library, as well as a house of healing where various injuries of life, from cuts and scrapes of children's play, to more critical wounds inflicted by work, and occasional ailments -- there had been no serious sicknesses in over two-hundred years -- were tended with practice and remedies ranging from ancient African to modern immunizations.

After mounting the steps to the wide front porch, Donte assisting Randy, Donte tugged up Randy's jeans.

"Thanks," Randy panted, wiping more sweat from his face. "Can't button 'em all the way no more."

"I can relate," said Donte, lifting his own roll of belly a bit to reveal two buttons undone on his cutoffs.

"I was always chubby," said Randy, but I got pretty out of shape this year."

"You are not pleased by your shape?" asked Thomas.

"Walter ain't, but you dudes make me feel good about me."

Donte smiled. "As Thomas said, we think you quite handsome."

Thomas laughed. "And for more than just your awesome belly."

Timothy knocked on the door, which was opened a few moments later by a chubby girl of Donte's age clad in blue shorts and a tight tank-top, both of which enhanced her lush figure rather than con-cealing it. Her skin was a velvety dusky shade, and her hair a raven halo of curls above onyx eyes that were large and long-lashed in a gently-rounded cheerful face.

Randy whispered in Donte's ear, "Woah, she's a fox! ...Is she your priestess?"

Donte murmured, "Damon's daughter, Tiya, though she will be our *Mambo* some day."

Thomas made kissy lips. "She is Donte's sweetheart."

"Shut up," Donte muttered.

"Lucky dude," whispered Randy.

The girl saw Randy and smiled, her chubby cheeks dimpling. "Welcome. I heard we had visitors, though I was occupied and could not come to the beach."

"This is Randy," said Donte.

"Hi," said Randy.

"You are," said Tiya, her smile turning sly.

"Huh?" said Randy.

Timothy chuckled. "Which is perfectly normal for a male of his age." Then his face turned serious. "May we see Damon?"

"Of course. A moment; she is consulting. Please come in."

Tiya stepped aside, and the boys filed in through the doorway, Donte still steadying Randy with an encircling arm. The house's front room was large and lofty, its tin roof lost in shadow above, with several rows of wooden benches suggestive of pews in a church but also fitted with surfaces to serve as schoolroom desks. As in Jean-Luc's house, one whole wall was devoted to books. There was also a blackboard -- actually black -- and a modern map of the world. Kerosene lamps hung from rafters, but none were presently alight, and the only illumination came from a triple scone of candles at the far end of the space. Donte noted Randy's eyes widen when he saw the altar. There, on a platform above the floor, softly lit by candle glow, was a trio of life-sized figures skillfully carved of ebony wood. One was of a skeleton clad like an old-time undertaker in a long frock-coat and tall top-hat, and holding a skull-headed walking-stick as if to go for a midnight stroll. While all skulls naturally smiled, both the one on the stick and its owner looked friendly. Beside him stood a beautiful woman of obviously African descent, dressed in an elegant evening gown in the style of centuries past and also smiling benevolently. One hand rested atop a shovel -- or rather an archaic spade -- suggesting that she and her grave com-panion had some earthy task to perform. Yet at the feet of this sepulchral pair lounged a naked fat boy of maybe eight who very much resembled Thomas, including an impish grin... except for a set of baby goat horns adorning his bushy-maned head. He was silently playing an African flute, though looking so real and full of life that one expected to hear happy notes.

"Are those your gods?" whispered Randy.

"They are the Trinity," said Tiya. "Both a trio and yet one... as Father, Son, and Holy Ghost... but to us a family, as we believe is God's true self." She indicated the figures. "The Baron Samedi, or as some say, Semetery, keeper of graveyards and guardian of the dead. His beautiful wife, Maman Brigette, and their son, little Ethu."

"What does he do?" asked Randy.

"What all children should. Would you like to meet Them?"

"...I don't have to die?"

Tiya laughed. "Rather you must *live* your life to its joyful fullest. Partake of all the good things in this world, and be thankful for them; yet do not let them enslave you into only wanting more and delude you to think they are all there is in an infinite universe. Dance all the way to your grave to the playful piping of Ethu, and know that death is only a door to another existence beyond." Taking Randy's hand, she led him to the altar.

"Randy *is* quite handsome," said Thomas, grinning very much like Ethu and giving Donte a nudge.

"Am I not?" asked Donte.

"One thing you are not," said Timothy.

"...What?" asked Donte.

"Our guest."

They followed Tiya and Randy to the candle-lit shrine. "He looks like Thomas," Randy was saying, indicating Ethu, while guided to kneel by Tiya as the other boys knelt behind them.

"Full of life," said Tiya. "And living it to its fullest, as all children rightfully should."

"Why does he have horns?"

"There are few things in life as joyful as kids."

"Or as randy," Timothy whispered, leaning to Donte's ear.

Randy lifted his eyes to Maman Brigette and the skeletal Baron. "Guess his parents love him a lot."

"As yours loved you," said a woman's voice. "And, still very much do."

Everyone turned as an impressive figure -- as black as space, Donte always thought, and as beautiful as the stars therein -- entered through a curtained doorway. Damon was clad in a blue cotton dress, her wrists encircled with copper bracelets. She wore a necklace of ruby glass beads, and a headband of feathers adorned her long hair. Her hand was upon the shoulder of a chubby boy of twelve, and she addressed him in Kreyol while indicating Ethu:

"He would not have empowered you so if you were not to enjoy it." She smiled and gave the boy a little blue jar of ointment. "But, perhaps a little less often until... as Donte might say... it is well run-in."

Donte smiled at the boy. "*Wi*, Laurent, as I learned myself."

Randy whispered in Donte's ear. "You talk about *that* in church?"

"It is a joyful part of life."

Randy smiled. "Works for me."

Laurent came to kneel at Ethu's feet, bowed his head and murmured, "*Mesi*," then rose and left the house.

Damon turned to Randy. "Your voyage has been pleasant?"

"It's been okay," said Randy, as Donte helped him vertical by hoist-ing him under the arms and tugged his jeans up again. "But, comin' here's been the best part. ...Is it true what you said about my parents?"

"Very much so," said Damon. "Though you do not have to trust my word, but feel for yourself their in your heart."

Randy touched his chest. "Sometimes I think I do."

"Your heart is what you must trust," said Damon. "Though there will be times of doubt. Times, perhaps, of troubled waters."

"I think I know what you mean."

Damon took Randy's shoulders. "You are a strong and good young man; rely on your strength an trust your heart and you will come through any storm."

Then she turned to Donte. "You wished to see me?"

Timothy said, "A feeling haunts him."

Donte nodded. "That there is... *something*... out on the sea. Have you not felt it?"

Damon looked thoughtful. "I did, this afternoon, sense a drifting loneliness." She smiled at Randy, though spoke in Kreyol. "But I assumed it was him when his vessel arrived, for *he* has been drifting and lonely."

"As I also considered," said Donte in English. "But, still this feeling haunts."

"Do you feel it is bad?" asked Tiya. "Threatening or malign?"

"...*Non*. Only that something is out there... perhaps even calling to me."

"That I do not feel," said Damon.

"Um, no offense," said Randy, "but I thought? ...I mean, you know Voodoo...?"

"I am but a voyager in life, as are we all who sail its sea. Sometimes the skies are clear, and there are stars to steer by at night. Other times there are clouds, or a mist obscures our vision, and we have only our compass of faith to guide us on the right course. And while, as in this, I have only my compass, perhaps Donte has mounted the mast and sees ahead what I cannot."

"Guess that makes sense," said Randy.

"Have you told your father, Donte?" asked Tiya.

"He said I should speak with Damon."

"What of the weather?" asked Damon.

"Clear, with gentle winds," said Thomas. "Though a slight fall of barometer."

Damon seemed to listen a moment, raising her head as Donte had done and looking toward the shimmering sea beyond a moonlit win-dow. "When does the schooner sail?"

"Full tide at midnight," said Timothy.

Damon faced Donte again. "Apparently, you *are* aloft, and I below in the mist. If you feel there is danger out there..."

"Only that there is... *something*," said Donte. "Lonely and drifting, perhaps, as you said."

36

"Your father is a wise captain. Tell him again what you feel, and he will make the right decision."

Donte nodded. "I will."

"You have done your duty, now be at peace." Damon took Randy's shoulders again and looked into his eyes. "Not all who drift are lost; some have only gotten off course until they sight a star to steer by... but one must always look for such stars. Remember to trust your heart in all things, for that is truest compass in life, and *bon voyage* wherever you sail."

"Thanks," said Randy.

Tiya accompanied the boys to the porch -- Randy now steadily underway without needing Donte's assistance -- and took Donte's hand for a moment as the others descended the steps. "You are also quite handsome," she whispered, and softly kissed his cheek.

SIX
Sis

"**A**re they gonna sail?" asked Randy, sitting in the long-boat, its flanks caressed by moon-silvered wavelets rippling up on the beach. Timothy filled the sternsheets again, while Thomas sat in the bow as Donte returned from the schooner.

"*Wi*," said Donte, pushing the boat off the sand and hoisting himself aboard. "I told my father as Damon advised, but there is no change in the weather report, the barometer not falling rapidly, and the tide is highest tonight for passage over the reefs... though he will keep a man on the mast to watch for any danger."

He took up the long heavy oars and swung the boat around, aiming her bow toward the anchored yacht in her bright electric aura, then paused to wave to his father, who stood at the schooner's helm as the crew hoisted sail and she came about, her running lamps glowing ruby and emerald, her canvas catching the breeze, filling, and heeling her a bit as she gathered way toward the mouth of the cove, her name, *Brigette*, revealed in the moonlight on her buxom stern.

The other boys also waved, but Donte began pulling stroke. "Do not wave a ship out of sight."

"How come?" asked Randy.

"Wave a ship out of sight, and you may never see her again."

"You sure know a lot about boats."

"We are a seafaring people, not only because of ancestry but also being islanders for the last three-hundred years."

"It may have been our sailors," said Thomas, "who first 'discovered' America."

"Though," added Timothy, "they did not plant a flag on the beach and claim it now belonged to them."

"But, nobody's ever sailed away? From you island, I mean, an' never came back?" asked Randy. "Like in storybooks where somebody goes to seek their fortune."

Timothy indicated the ocean beyond the rocky jaws of the cove. "As my father said tonight, we are aware of what is out there, and anyone may leave to seek it, but no one ever has."

"What about whoever got banished?"

Timothy gazed at the nighted sea. "That is a very sad story, and this is not the time to tell it."

The drone of the generator grew louder as they neared the yacht, though still muffled below deck, and probably insulated, thought Donte, to shield those aboard from discomforting sound. The vessel was not very far from new, constructed of gleaming white fiberglass, with decks of teak, mahogany trim, and railings and fittings of stainless-steel. She was graceful in a modern way, though seeming more suited to soaring through space than voyaging the oceans of earth; and Donte preferred more archaic designs, such as Little Orphan's schooner, built to actually live in the sea rather than only cleave its surface to get from one port to another.

Despite the humid heat of the night, every door and window seemed shut. Still, above the muffled drone, Donte heard the voices of Jason and Walter seemingly raised in argument as he guided the boat toward the big vessel's stern.

"You should make him go on a diet!" Walter was shrilling petulantly. "And get off his butt and get active! All he's done for a year is lay around and play video games while stuffing himself with unhealthy food!"

"See what I mean?" sighed Randy, as the longboat glided quietly closer.

"If that's what he wants..." Jason began.

"But he's not *healthy!*" Walter broke in, as if that word meant angelic perfection. "You let him eat junk and drink *sodas!* He was overweight to begin with, and now he's gotten *obese!*"

"Stop sounding like somebody's nagging mother! Or a bitchy wife!" snapped Jason. "And don't forget who's paying the bills!"

The voices cut off abruptly as Donte brought the boat alongside with a gentle bump. Thomas made their line fast to a cleat, and Donte boosted him up on deck, where he offered a hand to Randy and assisted him aboard. Then Thomas and Randy extended their hands, hauling Timothy up on deck, with Donte adding a push to Timothy's ample stern. Donte heard Jason's voice again, though now con-siderably lowered: "Did you lock everything?"

The afterdeck was canopied by an expanse of indigo canvas. There was a plastic table and chairs for, presumably, open-air dining; and the skiff had been hoisted back in its davits. Jason and Walter emerged from a doorway, both a bit red of face. Jason flicked Walter a warning look, then curtly beckoned to Donte. "This way."

Taking his tool pouch from Thomas, Donte slung it over a shoulder and, followed by the other boys, was led through the door-way by Jason into a large saloon cabin lit by glaring electric globes. Donte was momentarily blinded after being out in the night, and only got a dazzled impression of fiberglass walls and overhead as starkly white as cocoanut meat, a big mahogany table, settees upholstered in indigo plush, while his feet sank into blue carpeting as soft as forest moss. The air smelled of plastic and metal, and was colder than a winter night on Little Orphan's mountain. Slitting his assaulted eyes, he obeyed another beckon from Jason and followed him aft down a short companion into a carpeted passageway lined with mahogany doors, all shut. Except for these and woodwork trim, the corridor was also white and lighted brilliantly, which seemed to further intensify the blackness of Timothy, Donte and Thomas, while Randy was almost invisible like a ghost in fog. Randy followed Donte, trailed by Thomas and Timothy, while Walter brought up the rear as if he and Jason were jailers on a twenty-first century prison ship marching the boys to a cell. The air, as in the saloon above, was cold and metallically sterile; and the only hints of living things were the earthy scents of the boys. The men seemed to have showered and changed their clothes, and smelled somewhat antiseptic.

The drone of the generator grew louder as they descended

another companion to face an aluminum watertight door, and rose even more in volume as Jason threw back the dogs and swung the door aside, revealing a spacious engine room brightly lighted by bulbs. The interior was dominated by a pair of Caterpillar engines gleaming yellow under the lights. There were also two Onan generators, only one presently running, a thrumming air-conditioner unit, and various other machinery, including a desalinator. The air was comfortably warm to Donte, and familiar with the mechanical scents of diesel fuel and oil.

Donte turned to Jason and indicated the engines. "Which has been marching unwell?"

Jason looked annoyed, but pointed to the starboard.

"Describe the symptoms," said Donte.

"It started cutting out... sounded like it was missing... just before we saw your island. Then it died. We got it started again, but it didn't have much power. But it idled okay when we followed you in."

"May I hear it?"

"Walter, go up and start it."

"That is not necessary," said Donte. He affirmed the gearbox in neutral, then stepped to a little instrument panel on the front of the engine, adjusted a T-handle control, flipped a toggle switch, and pushed a rubber-sheathed button. The engine started instantly.

"I didn't know you could start it down here," said Jason.

"You have recently acquired this vessel?"

"A month ago," said Randy.

"We had another boat," said Jason, sounding slightly defensive.

"A *little* one," said Randy.

Donte inspected the idling engine, running a hand all over it as if to feel its pulse, and pressing an ear to its trembling flank before shutting it off. "I believe I know the problem." He unslung his pouch and spread out his tools on the aluminum diamond-plate deck.

Jason was looking doubtfully at the antique display. "You *do* know something about engines?"

Randy's voice was surprisingly sharp. "Don't bother him!"

Jason's cheeks flushed but he made no reply. Walter, however, began, "You know how much this boat...?"

"Who signed the check?" Randy retorted.

Both men frowned but said no more.

Thomas and Timothy seated themselves near a water heater, Timothy looking thoughtful and Thomas smiling impishly. Except for not having horns, Thomas looked more than ever like Ethu as he raised his flute to his lips. Timothy smiled at the men. "A little Voodoo to charm the repair."

Thomas began piping cheerfully, and Randy sat down beside him as Donte selected tools. Randy grinned. "Where's the pins to stick in the engine?"

"In this case a half-inch spanner," said Donte. "I also need a pan."

Randy gave Jason a look, and Jason went to a locker, returning with a black plastic pan of the type used to wash machinery parts. Donte loosened a bolt on a canister near the engine's fuel pump. Taking the pan from Jason, he drained fuel into it, then removed the canister and examined its paper filter.

"It is partially clogged," he said, and rubbed a paste-like substance between a thumb and finger. "This vessel being new, there is fiberglass dust in her fuel tanks. An obstructed fuel filter will often cause the engine malfunctions you described."

"...Oh," said Jason.

"Have you spare filters?" asked Donte.

"There should be," said Jason, going back to the locker. "The broker said she was fully fitted when we took delivery."

"It would have been wise to ascertain that before beginning your voyage," said Donte.

"...Yes. ...Here's one," said Jason, holding up a small box.

"Several spares would be prudent," said Donte, "before another voyage."

"I'll make sure of that," said Randy, with a glance at Jason.

"Have you wiping rags?" asked Donte.

"There's a bundle," said Jason, checking the locker again.

"One will suffice."

"So, that's all it was?" asked Walter, as Donte, taking the square of red cloth, strained fuel from the pan back into the canister, installed the new paper filter, then remounted the canister to the playful piping of Thomas.

"I believe so," said Donte. "Though I cannot say for certain without a sea-trial at speed. And, your other engine may suffer the same malfunction soon, though I can also service it with another filter."

"There was only one," said Jason.

"I can clean it," said Donte. "Which may be sufficient to reach Jamaica."

"Yes... please," said Jason. "And of course we'll pay you."

Randy smiled at Donte. "Mechanics charge a hundred bucks just to breathe on a boat in Miami."

"You are our guest," said Donte. "So there will be no fee."

"Er?" said Jason, as Donte went to the other engine. "Could you come back in the morning and go out with us to test the engines?"

"If you wish," said Donte.

"You dudes could stay here tonight," offered Randy, "so you don't have to row back an' forth."

"Er..." said Jason. "I'm sure they'd be more comfortable in their own beds and homes."

"Think they have cooties?" snapped Randy.

"Of course not," said Jason, cheeks flushing again. He glanced at Thomas. "But he's a lot younger, and I'm sure his parents..."

Thomas smiled at Randy. "We would be honored to be your guests."

Randy faced the men. "*I'm* sure Donte can finish the job without you watchin' him."

The men exchanged frowning glances, but Jason indicated the door and followed Walter out.

Timothy observed, "That was a powerful dismissal."

"Actually this is *my* boat," said Randy. "Jason got me to pay for it. Walter said this trip would be 'healthy' for me."

"Of course it is none of our business," said Donte.

Randy shrugged. "Jason an' Walter had plenty of money before I came to live with them... they're architects with their own company; got a big fancy house with a boat dock, an' a housekeeper an' cook. Jason gets an allowance from my dad's estate to take care of me, but

I have to approve any other expenses... like buyin' this boat. I have a financial advisor an' he wasn't happy about it, but Jason an' Walter said it would give me a 'new perspective.'"

"Has it not?" asked Donte, finishing with the port engine's filter.

"Except for bein' on a boat, it hasn't been much different from what I been doin' all year... which I guess ain't been much." Then Randy smiled. "Except for tonight; that's been really cool."

"Have you no friends in Miami?" asked Thomas.

"Ain't been goin' nowhere."

"School?" asked Donte, repacking his tools.

"On-line," said Randy. "With a tutor."

"Forgive me," said Timothy. "But, much of life is our own creation built from our hopes and dreams."

"I know what you mean," said Randy. "But I guess I don't have any dreams no more."

"Perhaps your uncle is right," said Donte. "This voyage may give you a new perspective."

"You dudes have, anyway." Randy got up and went to the door. "Want some pizza? ...Or, if you're tired...?"

"We are not that tired," said Thomas. "And we have never had pizza before."

SEVEN
Sèt

Randy, puffing, led the way up to the brightly-lit passage and stopped at one of the doors. "The hell...?" he panted, grasping the knob. Then he yelled, "Who locked this?"

Walter descended from the saloon. "Jason thought it might be a good idea. ...In case of engine fumes."

"Sure he did," said Randy. "Unlock it. ...An' all the others if they're locked, too."

Walter produced a ring of keys. "You just had dinner."

"An' now we're havin' a midnight snack," said Randy, as Walter keyed the door. "An' you don't have to sleep in separate cabins; they ain't gonna chop off your heads."

Walter looked startled, glanced at Timothy, Thomas and Donte, who merely smiled politely, then went down the passage unlocking doors.

Randy ushered his guests into a galley of white fiberglass and bright stainless-steel. There was a big electric range, plus a microwave oven, a double sink and counter-tops, and mahogany cabinets. There was also a large refrigerator; and he opened one of its double doors to reveal many shelves of frozen foods, most in colorful packaging displaying tempting "serving suggestions," though some looked rather improbable.

"I have seen magazine pictures of some of these," said Thomas.

"Jason an' Walter eat Jenny Craig," said Randy, reaching inside. "Since neither one can cook."

Donte laughed. "She must be very ample."

"She tastes like somebody ate her already an' spewed her back up. Sorry it's only frozen pizza, but this is the best, the Supreme Combo."

"Its picture is quite appetizing," Timothy said, regarding the box.

"Takes about fifteen minutes," said Randy. "I like 'em a little soft an' gooey... if that's cool with you?"

"I'm sure you have excellent taste," said Donte.

Randy patted his belly. "I guess it shows." Taking a knife from a drawer, he freed the pizza from plastic wrapping, set it on an aluminum platter and slid it into the oven. "Want a beer? Sorry it's only Heineken an' not as good as yours."

"I'm sure it is pleasing," said Timothy, accepting a bottle from Randy.

"Though not as full-bodied as ours," said Thomas, also accepting a bottle and taking a tentative sip.

"Manners," Donte reminded.

"He's right," said Randy. "An' your beer rocks. Wanna come in my room while we wait for the pizza?"

"That would be cool," said Thomas.

A few moments later Randy opened a door at the end of the passage, forward and beneath the saloon. "This is the Owner's State-room: Jason an' Walter have the Captain's Cabin."

The compartment was very large, Donte saw, its width the entire beam of the boat, with three portholes on either side curtained by indigo cloth. The sterile starkness of white fiberglass was softened by much varnished woodwork, including many lockers and drawers, a sizeable dresser with mirror, and comfortably cushioned settees. There was also a desk, on which sat a computer, a well-stocked liquor cabinet with a small sink and refrigerator, a digital stereo system, and an enormous television mounted on the aft bulkhead. There was a small shelf of books containing many children's classics - - *The Wind In The Willows, Winnie The Pooh, Alice In Wonderland, Kim*, and others -- obviously many times read. A vast mahogany-framed bed occupied most of the forward space, and could have accommodated four boys as fat as Timothy, with a mirror on the ceiling above. The carpeting here was thicker and softer than what had caressed Donte's feet so far; and even by American standards –

judged by pictures in magazines -- this was a princely palace afloat.

"This rocks!" exclaimed Thomas, gazing around.

Randy laughed. "Guess I look like Richie Rich, huh?"

Timothy smiled. "We have some of the comic books, and Richie has a good heart."

"Not my idea," said Randy, as Donte regarded the overhead mirror... which was a new perspective.

Despite its opulent luxury, the space was awesomely untidy; the carpet strewn with food packaging of the sort Walter would call "unhealthy"... potato chip bags and cookie boxes, candy bar wrappers and soda cans. There were also many Heineken bottles, empty cigarette packs, and evidence scattered here and there of copious pizza con-sumption. The bed had probably never been made during the week of the voyage, and its rumpled sheets were lavishly dusted with bits and crumbs of assorted snacks. If Randy possessed other clothing besides his ragged, outgrown jeans, it must have been stowed away; though there was a pair of tattered sneakers adrift amid the flotsam.

Still, unlike the rest of the vessel, the scents in here were of life -- very abundantly so, including boyish randyness -- though the air, at least to Donte, was on the edge of uncomfortably cool.

"Guess it's kinda messy," said Randy, plopping onto the bed and taking a gulp of beer, his torus of middle surrounding him. "Sit anywhere you want." He pointed to a door up forward. "That's the bathroom if you gotta go. There's two more in the guest cabins, if you wanna sleep in those."

Donte smiled. "The bathrooms?"

Randy laughed. "You dudes could stay here with me. There's plenty of room in the bed. ...'Course, I guess it smells."

Timothy settled onto the bed, joined by Thomas and Donte. "As you say, there is ample room, though I must warn you Thomas has cooties."

"I do not!" cried Thomas, and punched his brother's shoulder.

"I might have 'em," laughed Randy. "Ain't took a shower all week, like you probably noticed."

"You smell alive," said Donte.

Randy laughed again and made a fist-pumping gesture. "It's how I 'get active.' Like you might say, I'm well run-in."

"Practice makes perfect," said Timothy.

"Um, no offense, but how?" asked Randy. He stood up and hoisted two handfuls of belly, leaning far backward for balance. As Donte had already noted, its undersides were even whiter than the rest of him, and below a puff of chub spilled out of his mostly un-buttoned jeans, from which the pink tip of his shaft protruded.

"It's all there, but ain't much I can use. Guess that's full dis-closure... or not."

Timothy smiled. "I have not seen mine since I was eight, but with a will there is always a way."

"Yeah, I got a few ways."

"Does it not extend a bit more?" asked Donte, in technical cur-iosity.

Randy released a cascade of fat and held up a finger and thumb. "That's all I can do it with... that way."

"I, too, am a little chubby down there."

"But I guess you're bigger."

"That is mostly a myth," said Donte, slipping his cutoffs down.

"You're way less chubby than me," said Randy. "But we're about the same size."

"I still await Ethu's blessing," said Thomas, managing to display himself.

Timothy laughed. "You are welcome to look for mine."

"Wanna watch a movie?" asked Randy. "I got a lot of DVDs. An' a ton of games... all the ones my dad designed. He made 'em mostly for little kids... not a lot of violent stuff... but I play 'em anyway. Even designed a new one myself, an' it's sellin' good."

"Whatever you suggest," said Donte.

"*Have* you dudes seen movies?"

"Several times in Port-au-Prince, the last being *Finding Nemo*," said Thomas.

"I saw that when I was little," said Randy. "With my mom an' dad. Bought it on DVD this year."

Timothy said, "We would love to see it again."

"Sure," said Randy. "I'll get the pizza. There's more beer in that fridge. An' all that other stuff to drink. The bar was stocked when we got the boat, but we shoulda checked for fuel filters."

EIGHT
Wit

onte awoke to morning light filtering through curtained
portholes. The air was still a little too cool, whispering in
through louvered vents, though its alien chill was alleviated
by the warmth of Timothy's bulk at his back and Randy's softness
nestled to him like Christopher Robin might have hugged Pooh. A
dream still lingered in Donte's mind of embracing Tiya beneath a
palm tree in the pleasantly sun-warmed sand of the beach, their
bodies entwined, her breasts to his chest, while sharing what seemed
a timeless kiss -- though they had never yet done so -- and he would
have drawn away from Randy, whose soft boy-breasts *were* pressed
to his chest, while his pouty lips were suggestively parted, if not
wedged tight by Timothy. He felt a flush of embarrassment, and
another when spying the overhead mirror, which reflected two boys
embracing like lovers, but Timothy's mass prevented escape, and to
struggle would likely wake Randy; which might have been more
embarrassing since they had all slept naked -- there seeming no
reason for modesty after full disclosure – and, like most boys his age,
Donte usually wakened aroused. And, even more indelicately, his
shaft had quested into Randy's accommodating navel.

The vessel was pitching gently as small waves swept along her
hull with liquid whispering sounds, creating a motion of body to
body that Donte, despite his discomfiture, began to find not
unpleasant in what he supposed was natural in a purely physical
way, when Timothy murmured, "The wind is rising," and shifted his
mass sufficiently for Donte to make an escape.

"*Wi*," said Donte, sitting up. "And the reef is beginning to break."

"Huh?" said Randy, opening his eyes. "...Oh, good-mornin'."

"Good-morning," Donte replied, echoed by Thomas and Timothy.

Randy didn't seem aware of any nocturnal intimacy as he sat up and shook back his hair, though he smiled at Donte and said, "I usually wake up that way, too, but 'course on me it don't show. ...You were sayin' somethin' about the wind. Is there gonna be a storm?"

"Perhaps a squall," said Timothy, beginning his process of sitting up with Thomas's assistance. "It is too early for hurricanes, but we should consult your barometer before going to sea for a trail of your engines."

"I don't think we got one," said Randy. "There's a radio in the wheelhouse, an' we could listen to that. ...What if there is a squall?"

"You may wish stay in our cove for another day," said Donte.

"That's okay with me. It's cool havin' you dudes here. Wanna have breakfast?"

"Certainly!" said Thomas. "Will it be pizza?"

"If you want, but there's microwave breakfasts. They ain't as good as my mom used to make, but better than Walter's 'healthy' spew."

"Perhaps first we should hear of the weather," said Donte. He rose and went to a porthole, parting its curtains to view the sea beyond the mouth of the cove. Though it sparkled under the sun, distant clouds were tinted rose and drifting toward the island. "Red sky at morning."

"I've read that," said Randy. "'Sailor take warning.'"

A few minutes later and dressed again, the boys came down from the wheelhouse, which, Donte had noted, contained all the newest electronic devices for twenty-first century navigation. In addition to the radio, which Donte had tuned to the weather report, there was a radar, a GPS, and a fathometer... though no simple barometer.

"Merely a squall," said Donte, following Randy through the saloon, trailed by Thomas and Timothy. "Perhaps the sea will be calm by noon."

"Wish I could stay here awhile," said Randy.

Thomas said, "You are welcome to stay as long as you wish."

"That would be cool. But it's Jason an' Walter's honeymoon."

They filed down the companionway and into the gleaming galley, where Randy opened the fridge. "There's still a gallon of normal milk, not that crappy no-fat kind." He checked the date on the plastic container, then opened the cap and sniffed. "It's good. An' there's OJ, too."

"I see eggs," said Thomas.

"Yeah," said Randy. "An' sausages an' potatoes. I got 'em for myself. Mom taught me how to cook a little, but microwavin's easier."

Timothy offered, "I have some culinary skills, if you would like something besides from a box?"

"Cool," said Randy.

A short time later, the boys were seated in the saloon around the big mahogany table partaking of fluffy scrambled eggs with sausages and fried potatoes, along with buttered toast and jelly, accompanied by orange juice and milk, plus steaming mugs of coffee. The wind was growing stronger, and the rushing crash of breaking waves carried from the reefs, but the yacht rode easily to her anchor in the sheltered cove.

Donte had never had cow's milk before -- the milk on Little Orphan being supplied by goats – but rather liked the new flavor, as did Timothy and Thomas. The eggs were pale in contrast to those of the island's hens whose yolks were richly golden. And even Timothy's cooking skills, though rendering them sufficiently tasty, could not bring them fully back to life from a week of refrigerated interment. Timothy also had done his best to awaken the plastic-wrapped saus-ages and enliven the aging potatoes; and though all was palatable -- Randy digging in eagerly -- the best thing about this breakfast to Donte was, there was plenty of it.

Jason and Walter came up the companion, freshly showered and neatly dressed, both with mugs in hand. "Who made the coffee?" asked Jason.

"I," said Thomas.

"It's very good," said Walter.

Thomas shrugged. "I did my best, though finding no proper boiler, I had to resort to a teapot."

Jason looked surprised. "You didn't use the Mr. Coffee?"

"I could find only Folgers."

"Want breakfast?" asked Randy. "There's some left."

"No thanks to you, I'm sure," said Walter. "How many times have I told you, you need to lose weight?"

"Way too many."

Jason regarded the ocean, now turning gray beyond the windows as clouds rolled in to darken the sky. "Looks like it's getting rough out there."

Randy chomped buttered toast. "Donte said it's only a squall, but we should stay here till it's over."

Jason glanced at a clock on a bulkhead showing the time as near 7:30. "We're a day behind schedule already, and the rooms are booked in Kingston."

"So call the hotel an' say you'll be late."

"Can't get a phone signal," said Walter. "And we're out of radio range."

"So, we'll get other rooms. ...'We' can afford it, you know."

Jason frowned. "I'm not afraid of a little rough weather. Walter and I have been through a few storms... before you brought yours into our lives." He scanned the rolling sea again as raindrops started to speckle the windows. "The only thing I'm worried about is getting through those reefs."

"We are not worried," said Timothy, after drinking his milk.

Donte turned to Randy. "If you must go, we can pilot you out towing our longboat. Fifteen minutes at speed should be sufficient to test your engines, then we will return in our boat."

"Will you be okay?" asked Randy. "Those waves are gettin' big."

"We, too, have been through a few storms," said Thomas.

"Still," said Donte, facing Jason, "I advise you to wait until noon when the tide is highest."

"...I guess we can spare the time," said Jason.

Timothy smiled at Randy. "Would you like to come ashore? We can show you some of our island."

"Aboard our tractor," said Donte, "so walking will not be required."

"And we will have lunch," added Thomas.

"I like the sound of that," said Randy. "An' maybe we could see Ethu again? An' his mom an' dad?"

Timothy elbowed Donte and murmured, "And, of course, Tiya Millay."

NINE
Nêf

"**B**on *voyage*, Randy," said Tiya, taking Randy's hand as they stood on the beach by the longboat. "And stars to steer by at night."

It was a little past noon and the wind had lessened, though the sky was still darkly gunmetal gray, and warm rain falling steadily. Timothy lounged in the boat's sternsheets, while Thomas was coiling the bow line and Donte stood ready to launch. Tiya, again in her short cutoff jeans and blue tank-top -- the latter baring her soft roll of tummy and rain-painted tight to the spheres of her breasts -- had made a huge and delicious lunch of curried pork with rice and red beans, accompanied by glasses of fresh goat milk.

Randy, still holding her hand, asked, "Would you like to see the boat?"

Timothy grinned at Tiya. "*His* boat."

Randy turned to Donte. "If it's cool with you?"

"...Oh. Of course," said Donte.

"I would love to," said Tiya, also taking Donte's hand as both boys hastened to help her aboard.

The water in the cove was choppy, the boat pitching and rocking, her bow smacking up showers of spray that drenched all the kids aboard as Donte's strong strokes propelled them to the cheerful piping of Thomas' flute. There were still whitecaps out on the sea, and waves creaming over the reefs. Randy, sitting next to Tiya on the boat's second midships seat, sighed as they neared the yacht. "Wish I could stay here, like in a book, an' live happily ever after." He smiled at Timothy. "I'd probably get as fat as you."

Tiya touched Randy's chest. "Whatever shape you are happy in is the best home for your spirit in life."

"Guess everybody works on your island?"

"Everyone does what they do best, though of course we help each other with anything else that must be done."

"Guess I couldn't do much," said Randy. "Useful stuff, I mean. You don't need an expert on video games. ...Maybe I could shovel guano."

Donte made a face. "No one is happy doing that; it is just something that has to be done."

"You are welcome to stay," said Thomas, pausing in his piping. "And live with us happily ever after."

"That *would* be like in a story," said Randy. "Rich kid runs away from his money an' goes to live on an island."

Tiya smiled. "You did not say 'a primitive island.'"

"That's 'cause I don't think it is: you got everything you need."

Thomas asked, "Would your money not still be yours?"

"Guess it would," said Randy. "But I'm not like Richie Rich: I don't have a swimmin' pool full of it to load on a ship an' take with me. Most of it's in banks an' investments. Stocks an' bonds an' stuff like that. I just get a monthly allowance an' buy what I want with plastic or Paypal. I own my dad's company, so I'd have to keep in touch... consult with my financial advisor. Make decisions about business stuff. I'm good at pickin' games that sell."

"We get mail every month on our schooner," said Thomas, "from the post office in Port-au-Prince."

"A satellite phone?" Donte suggested. "With a solar charger."

"...Yeah," said Randy, brushing back his dripping hair as spray burst over the boat again. "But I'd *really* be like Richie Rich, always wantin' to help his poor friends... um, no offense."

Tiya said, "That is because he has a good heart."

"But they never take his money."

"That is because they have good hearts."

"Yeah, but that's in a story. In real life they probably would. Like, who'd wanna wear raggedy clothes if they had a rich friend to buy 'em new ones?"

"Why do you?" asked Tiya, palming Randy's pale knee bared by the rip in his jeans.

"These are the last jeans mom bought me."

Timothy said, "As you have observed, we need few clothes on Little Orphan."

"But, don't you want anything? ...Like a bigger cargo boat so you could sell more guano. An' with an engine instead of just sails."

"Engines require fuel," said Donte. "And its cost would nullify any additional profit. Even powering our tractor is becoming expensive. I have been considering converting it to burn coal, which is cheap in Jamaica since worldwide demand has been falling." He powerfully plied the oars as the boat's bow smacked another wave and spray drenched them again. "And the wind is always free."

"I'd still always wanna buy you somethin'."

"Your friendship would be enough," said Thomas.

"And that has no price," said Timothy."

"Wealth must complicate life," said Tiya.

"I been findin' that out this year." Randy gazed at the gray horizon beyond the mouth of the cove. "Out there you gotta think about money almost twenty-four-seven... what to do with it, how to make more, an' keep other people from stealin' it... an' I don't mean with guns. It's kinda like money owns *you* instead of the other way around."

"You are always welcome with us," said Thomas. "And whether or not you have money."

Donte guided them up to the yacht. "Perhaps you could stop and stay a few days when you make your voyage home."

"There probably won't be time... money takes time away from you, too."

Thomas made their line fast to a cleat, and Randy scrambled aboard to offer a hand to Tiya. Then Donte boosted Thomas, and all helped Timothy. Donte boarded last and drew the longboat around to the stern, securing her line to another cleat in preparation for towing. Faintly, carried aft on the wind above the generator's drone, he heard Walter's voice from the wheelhouse where a window was slightly open:

"I guess we couldn't leave him here? If that's what he wanted. And pick him up on the way back. He'll probably stay in his cabin again until we get to Jamaica, and he probably won't do anything there but lay around playing games and ordering from room service. It might be healthy for him on that island... like a fitness camp. At least they don't have junk food and sodas."

Jason's voice growled in return, "Too bad we can't leave him here permanently! ...But, what if he got sick or hurt? I wouldn't look like a good guardian, and his lawyer's been asking a lot of questions since we bought this boat."

"Would you have taken him in if he hadn't come with all that money?"

"What do you think?" snapped Jason. "He's a sullen little spoiled brat! ...And I'm sure you'd add 'obese' to everything else not to like about him."

"At least I've tried to like him."

"No you haven't," Jason retorted. "You've only been trying to make him something you're not ashamed to be seen with. ...Like a mother embarrassed by having a fat kid because it's politically-incorrect. We have five more years to use his money... that's all you have to like him for."

"If he doesn't die from living unhealthy."

"In which case I get all his money."

Donte glanced at his companions -- Randy escorting Tiya forward, Thomas and Timothy following -- but they didn't seem to have heard.

A few minutes later the anchor was hoisted by its electric winch, and the yacht was underway with everyone in the wheelhouse and Donte at the destroyer-style helm. Jason had been coldly polite when introduced to Tiya, Walter perhaps a bit warmer, and was peering ahead as windshield wipers battled the drumming rain. "You're sure you know the way?" he asked, as they approached the frothing reefs.

"I'm sure he does!" snapped Randy.

Still, the men looked uneasy as Donte piloted the yacht, now rolling and plunging, bow thrashing up spray, through a foaming gap in the jagged rock teeth. Beyond the reefs rolled long heavy swells, their crests still breaking shaggy white beneath the leaden sky, but the vessel rode them well as Donte opened the throttles and listened to the engines droning in duet below.

"What do you think?" asked Jason.

"I hear no dysfunction... from them," said Donte, advancing the throttles to three-quarter speed and guiding the yacht in a gradual circle to approach the reefs from seaward.

Randy asked, "Sure you can get back okay?"

Donte brought the yacht into the wind, lowered the throttles to idle and relinquished the wheel to Jason. "The wind is out of the west so it will be an easy row."

"Guess this is good-bye," said Randy, as a few minutes later he stood at the rail, his pale body glistening with rain, his long hair lank and dripping, while the other kids boarded the longboat.

"Return whenever you wish," said Timothy, settling onto the sternsheets.

"You are always welcome," said Thomas, taking his place in the bow.

"Wish it was that easy," sighed Randy, untying the longboat's line.

Tiya said, "Life may seem as complicated as our minds believe it to be, but your heart often sees the simplest and straightest course to happiness."

"Let your heart be your compass," said Donte, taking up the oars as Thomas drew in and coiled the line and the boat drifted away with the wind. "And *bon voyage* wherever you sail."

"And stars to steer by," added Timothy.

"Sure I can't give you some money?" called Randy. "I got a few hundred in cash."

"You have given us yourself," said Donte. "Someone good who we will remember. There is nothing more valuable."

"I'll always remember you, too," Randy called, as the longboat continued to drift downwind. "An' I won't wave you out of sight." He turned away, going forward, and disappeared through a doorway.

Jason, above in the wheelhouse, watched until the boat was clear. Then the engines throttled up with a puff of black smoke from the streamlined funnel, and, screws churning leaden water to cream, the yacht gathered speed and thundered away. Donte turned the boat toward the reefs and began to pull a steady stroke. Thomas took up his flute, but called, "I think the wind is shifting."

"*Wi*," said Timothy. "Coming around to the east. I will help you row." He maneuvered himself to a midships seat and took up a second pair of oars. Then Thomas pointed. "Look!"

The yacht was fading into the rain, but Randy had reappeared on her stern and was waving both hands. Donte and Timothy paused their rowing. Timothy said, "Perhaps more engine trouble?"

Randy leaped into the sea!

"MAN OVERBOARD!" yelled Donte, jumping up to face the yacht and cupping his hands to his mouth, but the vessel continued on, dwindling into the silvery rain and leaving behind the small bobbing gleam of Randy's golden hair.

"Come about!" ordered Donte, gabbing the oars and pulling hard with Timothy joining in. "Thomas! Tiya! Keep watch! Do not lose sight of him!"

The wind, shifted now almost fully astern, propelled them along as if to help, and in minutes they surged up to Randy. Donte backed his oars, while Tiya and Timothy grabbed Randy's arms and pulled him over the gunwale. He'd lost his jeans in the sea, and his hair streamed lank and bedraggled as he tumbled aboard like a rolly merboy to sprawl upon the gratings. He was panting for breath, but sat up and grinned.

"Never been much of a swimmer, but I float pretty good. ...Had the money in my pocket, but now I only have myself."

"Then you have all you need," said Tiya.

Donte looked after the yacht, now only a small white shape in the distance.

"They think I'm in my cabin," puffed Randy. "An' they won't miss me till they get to Jamaica."

"But, what then?" asked Donte.

"They'll think I got drunk an' fell overboard... almost did a few nights ago. But they won't be sad about it 'cause Jason will get my money."

"It may not be so simple..." Timothy began.

But, Donte turned toward the island, also vanishing into the rain as the easterly wind took them farther away. "At the moment we have other concerns."

"Mean we can't row back?" asked Randy.

"We have a gaff sail and a mast, but now the wind is fully off-shore and we must beat against it."

Thomas looked gloomy. "And will miss our supper."

"We have provisions," said Timothy. "There is a cask of fresh water, as well as smoked meats and dried fruit. And fishing gear, of course."

"Has this kinda thing happened before?"

Donte stowed the oars. "I was at sea for two days last year beating against a wind such as this. But we have a compass aboard so, even if we lose sight of the island we can still find our way home."

"Kinda like in that book," said Randy. *"We Didn't Mean To Go To Sea."*

"One of my favorite stories," said Tiya. "We have it in our library."

Randy looked down at himself. "Got any spare clothes, like jeans or somethin'?"

Thomas laughed. "You have your own ample loincloth. But I will make you another from a piece of our old sail."

"I will attend to that," said Tiya, reaching for a canvas bag stowed beneath a seat. Using a sailor's knife, she cut a rectangle of cloth from the ragged sail, then a short length of line from a coil. "Come stand before me."

Donte took Randy under the arms and helped him to his feet as the boat pitched and rocked on the shaggy-capped waves, and held his shoulders to steady him as Tiya fitted the loincloth beneath his bobbling belly.

"Notre beau garçon sauvage," said Tiya.

"Our handsome wild boy," Donte translated.

"I like the sound of that."

Timothy studied the sky. "This squall is moving on to the west, so there will be moonlight and stars to steer by."

"Kinda like what Damon said, huh?"

"...Perhaps," said Donte, and scanned the sea, gray and rolling under the rain, the yacht now long out of sight.

"You still feel that something is out there?" asked Tiya.

"*Wi*, and even more strongly."

TEN
Dis

"This stuff's pretty good," said Randy, as a few hours later with nightfall nearing, he gnawed a strip of smoked goat meat.

They had rigged the boat's sail and fitted her rudder; and Donte now sat at the tiller, an ancient box compass between his legs as the boat tacked heeling into the wind.

"But not as good as the supper we missed," Thomas lamented, while munching smoked fish.

"Will your parents be worried?" asked Randy.

"Concerned but not fearful," said Tiya, also partaking of fish. "All on Little Orphan are knowledgeable of the sea."

Timothy nodded while chewing goat. "They will have noted the change of wind and surmise what has happened to us."

"They also know our direction," said Donte. "And, if we are not back by morning, will send the fishing boat to find us." He scanned the gray empty ocean, the island no longer visible. Clouds still shrouded the gunmetal sky as dusk began to settle, and the rain was still falling, but the waves had ceased cresting white. "And now we are losing the wind, so will probably spend the night out here."

"This is pretty cool," said Randy, helping himself to more goat. "Like, this is *really* goin' to sea, not just layin' around on a yacht. ...Think you could teach me to sail?"

"Come take the tiller," said Donte.

"Good thing it's been rainin' all day," said Randy, coming to sit beside Donte, "or I'd be totally lobster."

Timothy finished his goat. "If we are not home by dawn we will make you a cape from the old sail."

"*Notre beau garçon* super-hero," said Tiya.

Randy laughed. "Thanks, but I don't think I'm very heroic."

"A hero becomes a hero when a hero is needed."

Donte placed Randy's hand on the tiller and indicated the compass. "Hold her on this course, but feel the wind on your face so you do not sail too close and jibe."

"Think I could learn your language?" asked Randy, while carefully watching the compass.

"Kreyol is simple," said Tiya. "More complex thoughts and descriptions of things we usually render in English or French."

"You know English already," said Thomas, "and can learn Kreyol and French in our school."

"Guess your school's pretty hard."

"Merely four hours a day in the morning, though we do not have a summer vacation... which originated in many countries, including the United States, so children could work on their family farms during the months of summer." Thomas laughed. "Which was not a vacation."

"But, all of you know so much."

"Perhaps because," said Tiya, "our school teaches what *should* be taught in a school... reading, writing, mathematics, science, our own history and that of the world, as well as natural history."

"Our time in school," added Timothy, "is not wasted by being 'taught' what our parents and elders have already taught us."

"And continue to teach us," said Donte, "by their experience and example."

"Guess there's a lot of homework?"

"None at all," said Tiya. "Except to learn from the life all around us... the land and sea, and our people; the animals, birds, and things of the sea; and to read at least one book a week."

Thomas laughed and patted his belly. "Nor is our time in school wasted by being told how much we should weigh, and we must conform to a dictated shape and hate and ridicule those who will not."

Tiya nodded. "We are taught *how* to think, not what to think."

"I like the sound of that," said Randy. "...So, I really could stay with you?"

Donte clasped a hand over Randy's to guide it on the tiller. "That was never in question."

"But," said Timothy, taking another strip of goat, "there may be complications which you have not foreseen. What will happen if you are not missed until your vessel reaches Jamaica? Your uncle will make a report to the authorities; and you are a person of wealth, so there will no doubt be a search back along your course, which may extend to our island."

"Couldn't you hide me?" asked Randy.

"If that is what you wish. But, as you said this afternoon, can you simply disappear?"

"Why not? I just won't be rich anymore. An' Jason will get my money... which was all he wanted." Randy turned to Donte. "Yeah, I heard 'em talkin' today, but I've heard that shit before. I'm just Jason's golden calf."

"Goose," corrected Thomas.

Donte said, "Walter seems to care about you."

"Maybe a little, but not who I am; only what he thinks I should be."

"We like you as you are," said Tiya.

"That's why I wanna live with you."

Timothy looked thoughtful. "I have read that when someone disappears and their body is not found, they cannot be declared legally dead until a number of years have passed; often seven in many countries, including, I think, the United States."

"So Jason won't get my money till seven years from now?"

"That is what I would guess, assuming you do wish to vanish, though my father will know."

Randy laughed. "Won't Jason be pissed!"

Donte gripped Randy's shoulder. "You must consider this carefully, and talk with Damon and Jean-Luc after we are home. ...For now, we should take down the sail and put out the drogue to slow our drift."

"I will rig it," said Thomas.

Donte regarded the ocean again: the clouds were beginning to break in the dusk, and the rain had softened to merely a drizzle. "Not many ships come this way, but we should light our lamp and keep a watch all night."

"Um?" asked Randy. "We're not in the Bermuda Triangle, are we? Like, we're not all gonna disappear?"

"That is far north-east," said Donte. "Though some have speculated that it probably has no well-defined limits but merely fades in phenomena farther away from its center."

"So, we're still near it?"

"Still far from what most believe are its borders."

The sail was lowered and furled; a lifeboat lantern was lighted with a wax-covered match and hoisted to the masthead, and the canvas drogue rigged to the bow line. The wind was now barely a breeze, and the waves only slow-rolling humps. The clouds continued to drift away, taking the drizzle with them, and the smile of moon materialized in the rapidly darkening sky.

"This is cool," said Randy. "You can see the stars comin' out... never paid much attention before." He laughed. "Too bad we don't have beer."

"There is a bottle of rum," said Thomas.

"Guess I gotta give up smokin'."

"There are homemade cigars," said Donte.

"You really do have everything. No wonder you don't need games an' TV."

Tiya smiled. "Life can be its best entertainment."

"'Specially when you got friends," said Randy, as Thomas gave him a slender cigar and fired another match. Randy puffed out a ghost of smoke, then took a sip of rum from the bottle Tiya passed to him. "How could there be any trouble? On your island, I mean? Like, what would anyone wanna do that was bad enough to get banished?"

Timothy's round face saddened in the silver glow of the smiling moon and golden lantern light. "The worst that one human can do to another."

"...You mean killin' somebody?"

Timothy also lit a cigar, held the match for Thomas, Tiya and Donte, then took a sip from the bottle. "As I said last night, a very sad story." He paused to study the star-sparkled sea, now growing glassy under the moon. "A triangle itself, as often called: in this case two men and a woman."

"Though not much older than we," said Tiya, "so one might say two boys and a girl."

"The boys loved the girl," said Donte. "And, it is said, she loved both of them and could not decide which to marry."

"So, one of the boys killed the other?" asked Randy. "Like in a story, to get the girl?"

Timothy passed the bottle to Tiya. "The evidence was circumstantial, since there was no one who saw what happened. And even our chief... my great-grandfather... was never sure he had made the right judgment."

"What did happen?" asked Randy.

Tiya passed the bottle to Thomas. "A trading steamer put into our cove. Her captain had heard we had guano and offered the Hornsby tractor in exchange for thirty tons. There was already close to that much waiting for shipment on the beach, but our chief sent the two boys up on the mountain to fill enough sacks to complete the tonnage, while the other men and boys were occupied loading the ship."

"But, the guano cliff collapsed," said Thomas. "And one of the boys was buried."

Timothy continued, "The other tried to dig him out, but finding the task too much for him, ran down to the village for help."

Donte accepted the bottle from Thomas. "That proved to be a fatal mistake, for had he continued to dig for perhaps another minute, the other boy might have been saved."

Randy turned to Timothy. "But you... I mean your great-grandfather... didn't think it was a mistake?"

Timothy exhaled a ghost. "He and the village elders, along with Tiya's great-grandmother, who was then our *Mambo*, examined all the evidence and deliberated carefully. The boy *had* clearly tried to dig the other out, but he'd been so *close* when he'd given up; so close that only a minute more would have uncovered the buried boy's hand so he could have been pulled out."

"Had he made a mistake," said Tiya, "and given up too soon?"

Donte passed the bottle to Randy. "Or, had he perhaps uncovered the hand, felt life still present, and *re-buried* it before running down to the village?"

"'Cause he had a motive," said Randy, "for wantin' the other boy out of his way so he could marry the girl."

Timothy nodded. "It was not an easy judgment to make, for though the boy's guilt could not be proved, neither could his innocence. And, in the pervious two-hundred years, no one on Little Orphan had ever slain another."

"Consider the dilemma," said Tiya. "A very small community on a tiny island, and no one would ever be certain there was not a murderer amongst them."

Randy asked, "Ever hear what happened to him after he got banished?"

"The steamer was short a stoker," said Thomas, accepting the bottle from Tiya, "so he signed aboard her. My great-grandfather did not tell her captain of his banishment, so he could begin a new life without taint."

"Beyond that," said Timothy, "we know nothing of what became of him."

"Guess the girl married somebody else?"

"*Non*," said Timothy. "She did not... or perhaps would not... believe that one of the boys she loved could have murdered the other, and waited in hope for the rest of her life that he might return with his innocence proved... often atop the mountain watching for his ship."

Tyia nodded. "It is said her spirit still waits for him there."

"It *is* a sad story," said Randy. He took a last puff of his cigar and flipped the stub into the now quiet sea. "Too bad she couldn't of married 'em both... but I guess that was against your law."

"It had never been done," said Timothy, consigning his cigar to the sea. "And so, I suppose, was never considered. We were not of an African tribe in which a man would have more than one wife. And there are not many cultures in which a woman may marry two men."

"But, you're open-minded," said Randy. "Like, you don't hate gay people."

Tiya cast away her cigar. "We have learned to accept new ideas if they are beneficial to us. To judge if new things will enable us to live happier lives in harmony with our spiritual beliefs, instead of only distracting us away from our families, friends, and God. Hate is also a distraction, and most destructive to happiness."

"So, you... I mean your great-grandparents... *might* have let 'em all get married?"

Timothy shrugged. "I cannot say what they might have done had such a marriage been proposed. But, there is no record of such a proposal, and something as notable as that would have been recorded."

"Maybe they were scared to ask?"

"Or perhaps," said Donte, "it did not occur to them."

"Or," said Tiya, "just not to the boys. Because they did not think it manly."

"...Yeah," said Randy. "Like, if the girl loved both of them, an' both of them loved her, they'd have to love each other, too, for somethin' like that to work."

"The irony," said Tiya, "was that they had been as close as brothers in their younger years."

"So, perhaps," said Timothy, "we were all responsible for this triple tragedy... one boy's death, another banished, and a girl alone for the rest of her life... because we were not enlightened enough to acknowledge such a love."

"What would you have done?" asked Randy, "if you'd been chief an' *Mambo* then?"

Tiya and Timothy said together, "The right thing, I hope."

Randy looked up at the sky. "Never knew there were so many stars."

"So much beauty," said Timothy. "For all on earth to cherish."

"Does that include ghosts?"

Tiya smiled. "Why should it not? ...Thomas, will you play for us?"

ELEVEN
Onz

"**D**onte," whispered Thomas, crouching close to Donte's ear.

Donte opened his eyes to silver starlight and the golden glow of the lamp on the mast. He'd been dreaming of breasts softly pressed to his chest, and found Randy nestled against him on the old sail they'd spread on the gratings, while Timothy slept on the sternsheets and Tiya in the bow. They had stayed awake until midnight singing songs to Thomas' piping, then Thomas had taken first watch.

Drawing gently away so he wouldn't wake Randy, Donte sat up to scan the stars, and noted the Cheshire smile of moon, now ghostly blue and low in the west. "Time for my watch?" he yawned.

But Thomas pointed toward the moon. "Look."

Donte gazed across the sea, shimmering silent and nearly dead calm. Almost at the edge of sight, he saw a dark shape on the glistening moon-path. "A ship," he whispered. "Not very large, and showing no lights."

"There is a glimmer."

"Probably just the moon reflecting from a porthole," said Donte, after another moment of study. "Or a wheelhouse window." He stood up and shaded his eyes from the stars. "There is no smoke from her funnel. Perhaps she is having engine trouble. How long has she been there?"

"I sighted her a short time ago as the moon was lowering. At first I thought she was coming this way, but she has not moved. Though I think we are drifting toward her."

"...Perhaps," said Donte, still scanning the shadow-shrouded ship and noting another faint glimmer. "There may be a current." Then he shrugged. "We do not need her help. There will be wind after dawn, and we should be home for supper."

"Perhaps she needs our help?" said Thomas. "She looks very lonely somehow."

"Those aboard should have seen our lamp, yet they have made no signal," said Donte. "Perhaps they are simply hove-to for the night, it is too deep here to anchor, though they should be showing mast lights."

"Or, perhaps they are all below trying to repair her engine?" Thomas also shaded his eyes and regarded the distant ship, now becoming silhouetted against the blue glow of the lowering moon as if materializing out of an ethereal mist, her two tall masts pointing spectrally skyward. "And I think she faces away from us, so maybe we haven't been seen. ...It would not be a lengthy row to her. And, if you could help them with your skills, perhaps they might offer us break-fast."

Timothy sat up ponderously to also study the ship. "They could be smugglers or pirates. Perhaps we should row... but away! And put out our lamp before we are seen."

"What's up?" asked Randy, also sitting, and brushing his hair out of his eyes. He turned where the other boys faced. "I hope that's not my boat comin' back lookin' for me!"

"*Non*," said Donte. "She is over twice the size and of much older design. Probably a freighter."

Timothy said, "Which could be smuggling drugs and does not want to be seen. ...You are captain, what are your orders?"

Donte continued to study the ship... the longboat did seem to be drifting toward her. "Perhaps," he said at last, "she is what I have felt since yesterday up on our mountain... something lonely and drifting out here."

"But, not bad?" asked Tiya, coming aft to join the boys.

"I cannot tell. What do you feel?"

Tiya gazed at the ship for a time. "Nothing more than you describe... a sad and lonely drifting."

"So, perhaps she does need our help," said Thomas.

"We have nothing for pirates to steal," said Donte. "Nor should we be of concern to smugglers, for who could we tell who would trouble them."

Randy asked, "You sayin' we should check her out?"

"There may be, as Thomas proposed, a chance of earning breakfast if there is any help we can offer."

"I like the sound of that."

Donte offered a hand, assisting Randy to his feet. "And possibly a pair of jeans for our *beau garçon sauvage*."

"That would be cool," said Randy. "'Least I'd have somethin' to start my new life."

"What you already have is sufficient," said Tiya.

"Thomas, bring in the drogue," said Donte. He moved to one of the middle seats and unshipped a pair of oars, while Timothy took the other pair.

"Can I do somethin'?" asked Randy.

"Take the tiller," said Donte, "and hold our course for the ship. Tiya, please sit beside him for trim."

"With pleasure," said Tiya, joining Randy.

They started across the glassy sea along the shimmering moon-path, the only sounds the creak of oarlocks and the liquid whispering of water cleaving to the bow. There did seem to be a current drawing them toward the shadowy ship, because, glancing over his shoulder, Donte saw they were nearing her more swiftly somehow than they should.

"She does face away from us," said Thomas, standing in the bow. "And she is listing a little to port. And her head is somewhat down."

"Mean she could be sinkin'?" asked Randy.

Donte looked over his shoulder again. "If so, it is very slowly. Her loom has not changed since we first sighted her."

"Perhaps she has been abandoned?" said Tiya. "That would explain her showing no lights."

"There is no boat in her davits," said Thomas, still peering ahead and shading his eyes. He added as they continued to near, "She is very old. I have only seen pictures of ships that old."

"And very rusty," said Tiya. "There seems not a trace of paint left upon her."

Donte looked over his shoulder again. "She is a steamer; her funnel so tall to draw boiler draft. I, too, have seen only pictures of ships as old as she."

The ship was looming over them now, showing a high and graceful stern, her massive rudder centered, and a tip of propeller blade exposed above the glassy water. She was clearly an ancient cargo steamer, of riveted iron construction; a "three-island" type with high bow and stern, and cabin and wheelhouse amidships, along with a towering funnel, and tall cargo masts fore and aft. As Thomas had observed, she listed a little to port, and her bow was down by maybe a meter.

"She sure *is* rusty," said Randy. "An' look at all the seaweed an' barnacles."

"Pause," said Donte, shipping his oars as they glided out of the moonlight into the old vessel's shadow. Timothy also drew in his oars as Donte stood to study the ship, gazing up at the dark wheelhouse, where only a glimmer showed now and then of starlight reflecting from glass. Without the sounds of rowing, there was only the lapping of water along the ship's massively barnacled hull where ropes of seaweed slowly swayed in an aura of pale luminescence.

"Why is it glowin' down there?" asked Randy. "It's sorta spooky woo woo."

"From all the sea-life upon her," said Donte.

"A derelict," said Timothy. "And she must have been drifting for years."

Donte gazed up at the rust-eaten plates and salt-crusted wheelhouse windows. "Much longer than that I would say."

Tiya asked, "But how could that be possible? Surely she would have been discovered."

"*Wi*," agreed Timothy. "There are thousands of fishing vessels, freighters, cruise ships, tankers and yachts plying the Caribbean; surely some would have sighted her and reported a hazard to navigation."

Donte still studied the silent ship. "Yet, it would seem she has not been discovered. ...And do we know she is abandoned?"

"I would say at least by the living," said Tiya.

"Huh?" said Randy. "You sayin' there might be ghosts on this ship?"

Tiya cupped her hands to her mouth. "AHOY ON BOARD!"

Only the soft sea sounds replied.

Randy shivered a little. "Did you expect an answer?"

"I did not think it impossible."

Donte asked, "Do you feel there may be spirits aboard?"

"I still feel nothing more than you... and perhaps that is only her loneliness."

"...Huh?" said Randy again. "You mean the ship? ...But it's just a bunch of rusty old metal."

"Things may also have spirits," said Tiya. "Things that are naturally born of this earth, and things that have once been a part of lives, intimately involved with lives. Such things may become instilled with life and endowed with a spirit of their own... a good spirit if those lives were happy." She paused in thought for a moment. "Donte has an affinity with machines and mechanical things, which may explain why he felt her first and more intensely than I or my mother."

"...Guess that makes sense," said Randy. "...Could we go around to the other side? It's kinda creepy here in the dark."

Donte nodded. "I see no way on this side to board her; it is five meters up to her cargo decks."

"You wanna go aboard?" asked Randy. "This spooky old ship?" Then he laughed. "I don't think we're gonna get breakfast on her!"

"But, assuming she is abandoned," said Donte, "by law she may be claimed and salvaged by anyone who finds her."

Timothy added, "We have no way to take her home... that would require a tug... but there may be useful things aboard."

"An' maybe jeans," said Randy.

Donte and Timothy took up their oars and rowed to the old ship's straight-stemmed bow. "She still has her anchor," said Timothy. "Too bad her name has rusted away."

"There may be documents on board. ...Pause," said Donte, shipping his oars, then reaching to touch the ship's rusty stem.

"What do you feel" asked Tiya.

"...Only loneliness."

They continued around to the starboard side, emerging into moonlight again. "Could she be sinkin'?" asked Randy.

"I am amazed she is still afloat, being so sadly rusted," said Donte. "But she rides no lower than when we first saw her. Her list may be due to shifted cargo, and her lowered head caused by rainwater in her forward bilges. I doubt her hatches are still weather-tight."

"There is a line overside," said Thomas.

Donte saw a frayed bight of hawser dangling out of a scupper along the forward cargo deck. But, it was well out of reach, he found, after mounting the longboat's gunwale and stretching up his arms.

"I see nothing else," said Timothy, scanning along the ship's rusty flank.

"The sounding line, Thomas," said Donte.

Thomas produced a length of light line with a weight attached to one end. He heaved it expertly, the weight sailing though the hawser's bight and dropping back down the ship's side with a clatter. Then he tied on a heavier line and hauled it up through the bight.

"I get it," said Randy. "Donte can climb to the big rope on that."

"Hawser," Thomas corrected. "And there are no ropes on a boat, only lines."

"Okay, got that, too," said Randy.

Donte tugged on the line. "Assuming the hawser does not pull out, or is so rotted it breaks."

"I'm too fat to climb that," said Randy.

"As am I," said Timothy, and was echoed by Thomas.

"I will come after you, Donte," said Tiya. "Together we can hoist Randy; the three of us can lift Thomas, then all of us will hoist Timothy."

Donte cupped his hands to his mouth. "AHOY! WE ARE COMING ABOARD!"

"What if you woke up a ghost?" said Randy.

Tiya said, "Spirits will already know we are here. As does hers, if she has one."

Donte added, "But, there may be someone alive on board. Some-one else may have already found her, and to establish a salvage claim someone must remain aboard."

He waited another moment, but again only sea sounds replied to his hail. Then, slinging his tool pouch over a shoulder, his chest and arm muscles revealing themselves beneath their padding of chub-biness, he climbed the ship's side to the hawser and clambered over the bulwarks.

There are few things sadder to see than the rusted decks of abandoned ships with wheelhouse windows like empty skull eyes staring hollowly down, and Donte took only a moment to scan the spectral scene, noting heavy plank hatch covers with only shreds of canvas remaining. But, aside from the ghostly desolation, something didn't seem right; and though he didn't know what it was, it haunted his mind as Tiya climbed up and he assisted her to the deck. Then, together, they hoisted Randy.

"This is spooky woo woo!" puffed Randy, staring up at the black empty windows.

"In abundance," Donte agreed. "But, if there is something to fear, it might be someone living aboard who guards the salvage rights."

"Think there might be?" asked Randy, as Donte lowered the line to Thomas. "Even if they were sleepin', they shoulda heard us by now."

"It does seem doubtful," said Donte. "There should be lamps at the mastheads if anyone has claimed her." Then he called to Thomas, "Heave our bow line."

Donte caught the longboat's line, drew it through the scupper, and made it fast to a massive cleat. Then he, Tiya and Randy hoisted Thomas aboard. Finally, with the four of them pulling, Timothy, bringing the lantern, was also hauled aboard. By now the moon was below the horizon, leaving only pale starlight, but Timothy scanned around.

"This is not right," he said.

"Something is not," said Donte. "But I cannot bring it to mind."

"What is not here that should be?" said Tiya.

"What do you mean?" asked Thomas, gazing across the desolate deck.

"What is atop our mountain?"

"Bird shit!" said Randy, snapping his fingers. "Jason's always bitchin' about seagulls shittin' on 'his' boat."

"*Wi*," said Donte. "Her decks should be deeply covered with it from years of resting birds."

"I don't even see one splatter," said Randy.

"Which is strange," said Tiya. "Where could she have been all this time and not have had sea-birds aboard her?"

"The middle of the ocean?" said Randy. "Like, the Atlantic, I guess?"

"Even there birds would have found her," said Donte, "and come to sleep and rest."

Tiya nodded thoughtfully. "Unless there is something about her they fear."

TWELVE
Douz

"**W**here away, Captain?" asked Timothy.

"It would seem the first thing," replied Donte, "is to make sure there is no one aboard. There should be a captain's sea-cabin in the after part of the wheelhouse. That is where I would stay if I were guarding salvage rights so I could have a good view from the bridge of any vessels approaching."

"Um?" asked Randy. "We're not gonna do like in movies, are we? Split up an' go lookin' around so the guy with the axe kills us one at a time?"

Donte laughed. "I am familiar with that plot; and since we are not dim-witted teens, we will stay together. Tiya will deal with spirit en-counters, but we should probably arm ourselves against any physical threats." He pointed. "Those capstan bars should suffice."

"Unless he's got a gun," said Randy.

"This is not the United States."

Everyone went to a rack on the front of the superstructure, which held a row of iron bars, each well over a meter in length, and solid despite being heavily rusted. The boarding party thus equipped, and following Donte, who'd taken the lantern, they filed up the steep, narrow stairs to the bridge. Being only a small cargo vessel, the wheel-house was maybe five meters wide and extended roughly twice that length ahead of the lofty funnel. Its doors to the bridge, starboard and port, had obviously not been opened for many more than a few decades, and their latches, through bronze, were greenly seized.

Timothy puffed, out of breath from the climb, while inspecting a latch, "No one could be in there."

"At least with their skin still on," panted Thomas.

Tiya pressed her cheek to the door. "I feel no spirit presence."

"There may be documents in the sea-cabin that would tell us her name," said Donte.

"Break a window?" Randy suggested, also puffing from the climb.

Though that seemed the most logical course, Donte felt a reluctance to harm the ancient ship. He drew a small pry bar from his pouch, and while Tiya held the lantern, jemmied the latch until it released. Then, with Randy helping, they wrenched the door open on hinges that screamed, the shriek rendered even more ghastly by echo-ing in starlit silence over the empty sea.

A dank mustiness wafted out in their faces, and the lantern flickered and dimmed as Donte held it high and peered in. As with most small ships of her time, her steering was mechanical, of the rod-and-chain type with steam assist, and her wooden-spoked wheel was enormous, its diameter more than Donte's height. There was a green-crusted brass binnacle housing a massive magnetic compass with two iron compensating balls, an engine room telegraph pedestal, a speaking-tube to the engine room, and a dangling chain for the siren that slowly swayed to the long ocean swells, to which the ship rode on her starboard beam. Donte paused for the air to clear, then, trailed by his companions, padded to the telegraph.

"All Stop," he said, indicating the dial.

"Ain't that logical?" asked Randy. "If everybody abandoned ship?"

"Only if they did in haste. It should read Finished With Engines, as she certainly is." Giving the lantern to Timothy, he pulled the handle to that position. From somewhere deep in darkness below a faint bell jangled eerily.

Randy jumped. "Spooky woo woo, man! Felt like a *skeleton* touched my back!"

"*Wi*," said Thomas, hugging himself. "No more such frights without warning, please!"

"Then be warned," said Donte. He opened the cap of the speaking-tube and blew into the cone. From far below a faint whistle sounded, as eerie as the jangling bell. Then he called into the cone,

"Is anyone standing by?"

Randy shivered in the night heat, "Are you *tryin'* to wake up a ghost?"

Donte put an ear to the cone. "None are answering."

"That is sufficient spooky woo woo." Timothy went to a large table aft and held the lantern above it. "Here is the chart I assume they were using when she was abandoned."

Leaning close in the flickering glow, he scanned what lay pinned to the table as Donte and the others joined him. Careful of the brittle old paper, he traced a chubby finger along a faded pencil line. "This was her last recorded position, north-by-northeast of the Turk Islands and seemingly bound for Bermuda."

Randy asked, "Does that mean what I think it does?"

"She was in the Triangle," said Donte.

"Think that stuff is true? Ships an' airplanes disappearing into time warps or other dimensions?"

"She has been somewhere all this time, and has remained undiscovered," said Tiya. "Even, it would seem, by birds."

"If not for that," said Timothy, "one might speculate she was lying aground, perhaps on some deserted island, and only recently floated free."

"So, she *coulda* been trapped in the Triangle?" asked Randy. "An' finally drifted out? ...Or maybe *it* let her go?"

"I did feel her first, from up on our mountain, to the north-east of our island," said Donte. "And there is a current making south-west that could have carried her past that night. And the westering squall yester-day. Those could have brought her to where she is now."

"You said the Bermuda Triangle is north-east of your island." Randy studied the chart. "An' that's the direction she came from."

"Still," said Timothy, "even if we consider that she was somehow trapped somewhere, time must have passed wherever it was, for she looks every day of a hundred years old and obviously not preserved."

"I would say even older," said Donte. He pointed to a kerosene lamp swaying in gimbals over the table. "She is not electrically fitted, as most steamers were by the first decade of the twentieth century. From what I know of her type from books, I would say she was built in the 1890s. This chart is dated 1912, and was probably fairly new when she made her last voyage."

"Then," said Thomas, "at least a hundred years have passed since she was abandoned."

"This chart is in English," said Timothy. "Which tells us something about her."

"Shouldn't there be a log book?" asked Randy.

"Those are usually taken," said Donte, "when abandoning ship. As are important documents, assuming there is time." He indicated a narrow door to starboard of the table. "There is the captain's sea-cabin, and there should be something inside that might at least give us her name."

The doorknob, though reluctantly, turned in Donte's grasp, and the hinges gibbered as he pushed the door open, releasing another musty miasma, and again the lantern flickered and dimmed. A pair of salt-crusted portholes aft, glowing from the starlight, stared like milky dead man's eyes. Then the lantern began to recover, and Donte held it high. The slowly waxing flame revealed a typical captain's sea-cabin on an early twentieth-century steamer. Donte's eyes went first to the bunk -- made of oak and built into the wood-work, with drawers for stowage underneath -- but there was no skeletal occupant.

The rest of the cabin's furnishings were also in keeping with a vessel built in the late Victorian Age: there was a desk, also of oak, its chair restrained from wandering by a clamping device, a tarnished lamp in gimbals above, and shelves with puffy, mold-shrouded books, a few burst open like small bloated corpses. There were lockers and cabinets, several with doors swaying ajar to the slow-rolling pulse of the sea.

"It would seem," said Tiya, trailing with Randy as Donte entered, "she *was* abandoned in haste."

"*Wi*," agreed Donte, gazing around. "Though, it would seem, not during a storm."

"What makes you say that?" asked Randy.

"There are the captain's sea-boots," said Timothy, squeezing the mass of his middle through the narrow doorway.

"And his oilskin," added Thomas, entering after his brother.

Donte looked into a locker. "And these garments left behind... or what remain of them... are all for cold or hostile weather, so we may assume it was summer, and clear."

Randy came up beside Donte and touched a pair of rotted wool trousers, his fingertip going right though. "There's nothin' in here I can wear, an' I guess jeans weren't invented yet."

"But they were," said Timothy. "In 1871, by Jacob Davis and Levi Strauss, though Levi gets all the credit."

"There may be dungarees," said Donte, "in the crew quarters below."

"Old-school jeans," said Thomas.

"And possibly in better condition, less exposed to the atmosphere."

Randy smiled at Tiya. "This loincloth you made me is cool, but I kinda miss havin' pockets, even if I got nothin' to put in 'em."

Tiya smiled back. "One does need a few bare essentials."

Timothy went to the desk. "The captain must have taken the log, and probably her documents, though there may be other papers in his cabin below."

"The captain had two cabins?" asked Randy.

"*Wi*," said Donte. "This sea-cabin was mostly used when he wanted to be near the helm, such as during a storm or in other hazardous times."

Timothy opened one of the drawers, searched though some pulpy old papers inside, and finally held one up to the light. "Most of these cannot be read, but here is a cargo consignment... twenty cases of Barbancourt rum taken aboard in Port-au-Prince for shipment to Bermuda in June of 1916."

"Someone had good taste," said Tiya.

"Is this the stuff?" asked Randy, taking a bottle from a rack of others. "The label's almost gone."

"*Wi*, that is Barbancourt," said Thomas. "One of the finest rums in the world."

"Think it's curdled by now?"

"Most liquors do not go bad with age, and many improve," said

Tiya.

Randy uncapped the bottle and sipped. "This is pretty good."

"Indeed," said Thomas, joining him.

"Does it give her name?" asked Donte, holding the lantern close as Timothy tried to decipher the spidery, time-faded fountain-pen writ-ing.

"*S.S. Dorrit Foxley*, a very British-sounding name. As is her captain's, Jonas Grumby. ...*Wi*, her home port, Liverpool."

"At least she will not die nameless," said Donte.

"Mean she's gonna sink?" asked Randy.

"As I said when we arrived, I am amazed she is still afloat. I cannot imagine where she has been or how she has survived this long, but judging from her present condition she cannot live much longer, and a sizeable storm will surely sink her." Donte studied a brass barometer mounted above the desk. He tapped it with a fingertip and its needle quivered. "Assuming this still works, she may be safe for a day or so."

"From storms?" asked Randy.

"This foretells calm weather, though there may be rain."

"But, couldn't you use a lot of this stuff? All the people on your island?" Randy indicated the cabin lamp. "Like this?"

"*Wi*," said Timothy. "There are no doubt many lamps aboard, as well as other useful things."

"And surely tools," said Donte, "in the engine room." He made a wry face. "And shovels, for which we have obvious use."

"And her cargo," said Thomas. "Besides the rum, of course, there may be other valuable things."

Timothy said, "Since we cannot take her home; and assuming no one is aboard who has already claimed the salvage rights..."

"Which we will soon ascertain," said Donte.

"...we will establish a claim." Timothy squeezed himself back through the doorway, going out on the portside bridge to scan the starry sky. "It will be dawn in about two hours," he said as the others joined him. "And there should be a westerly wind to take the long-boat home. We will load her with things most useful to us... lamps and lanterns, cooking utensils, tools, and whatever else she can bear.

We may meet our fishing boat on the way back, probably captained by Andre with perhaps Laurent as crew; if so we will send them on to salvage other valuable things." He paused to finger the rusty rail. "And if *Dorrit* stays afloat we can bring the schooner to salvage more when she returns from Port-au-Prince."

Randy asked, "But, doesn't someone have to stay on board?"

"I will stay," said Donte.

"But, what if she starts sinkin'?"

"As the barometer indicates, there is at least one day of calm weather." Donte pointed to the foredeck. "And if she simply gives up and sinks, one of those timber hatch covers would make a substantial raft. And our boats will come searching for me."

"Damn! If I could get to a phone I could get a tugboat for you. ...How much do they cost?"

"I assume you mean to charter, not buy? At least, in United States money, a thousand dollars a day."

"That wouldn't be a problem."

"But," said Tiya, "then you would be revealing yourself."

"...Oh, yeah, I forgot I'm supposed to be dead. ...Well, I'd do it anyway 'cause you're all my friends."

Timothy laughed. "The term, I believe, is 'group hug.'"

Randy was engulfed by the others, and blushed a bit in the starlight as Tiya added a kiss to his cheek.

Then Timothy said, "Though we are certainly grateful that you would offer such kindness, the point at present is moot, since we do not have any means to communicate with the world."

Randy turned to Donte. "Let me stay with you."

"I would welcome your company."

"What are your orders, Captain?" asked Thomas.

"We should hoist lamps to mastheads to show that she is no longer abandoned." Donte paused to scan around. "But I see no lights of other vessels, and soon it will be dawn. For the present we should continue our search for anyone else aboard, who would surely have to be soundly asleep not to have heard us by now."

"Maybe they found the rum," said Randy.

"Or maybe they think we're pirates," said Thomas, "and are hiding from us."

"Ahoy!" called Tiya. "To anyone here, we mean you no harm!" She repeated her entreaty in French, then again in Kreyol.

Then Randy called, *"Ningú daño te!"*

"You speak Spanish?" asked Tiya.

"Only a little. Jason's cook is Cuban, an' I been helpin' her learn English."

Then everyone fell silent to listen, but only the soft sea sounds replied.

THIRTEEN
Trèz

"**F**rom stem to stern," said Donte. "Though, with her hatches still battened I doubt anyone could be in the holds."

Randy pointed forward. "Isn't that called the forecastle... that high part in the bow? Where the sailors lived?"

"Pronounced 'fo'c'sle' in English," said Donte. "But only on sailing ships. After steamers came into being, laws were passed forbidding crew quarters forward of the collision bulkhead. Now it is properly called a forepeak, and generally used for stowage... though someone could be inside."

Still armed with the iron bars, they descended to the cargo deck, passing the two hatch covers and the lofty mast, its booms upraised like skeletal fingers as if to grasp the stars, to arrive at a watertight door in the forepeak. Donte tried one of its four rusty dogs, then examined the others. "This has not been opened for decades, and we will need much heavier tools than I posses to open it."

"That porthole is open," said Randy, pointing.

Donte went to a circle of blackness about eye-level to him. "I would say this has been open for as long as the door has been shut... the deadlight is solidly rusted and the hinges seized. And I could not fit though it... a boy of Thomas' age perhaps, but surely no one older."

Thomas laughed. "A much slimmer boy of my age."

Returning to the midships section, Donte jemmied another corroded latch and, with Randy helping, pulled another door open to darkness on eerily creaking hinges. Again, a dank, musty breath wafted out, making the lantern flicker and dim, and he waited for it to re-cover, then held it high and leaned in. "The mess room and galley."

The compartment was maybe ten meters by ten, though split athwartships by a bulkhead with a doorway and a serving hatch into separate spaces for cooking and dining. The latter, which Donte now entered, contained a long table with benches attached and bolted to the rusty deck. Two lamps in gimbals swayed overhead amongst dang-ling scabs of peeling paint, once white but now yellowed like long-buried bones.

"Looks like they left in the middle of breakfast," said Randy, trail-ing, along with Tiya, and followed by Thomas and Timothy.

The table was still set with crockery of heavy utilitarian type -- mugs and plates, a service for ten -- along with age-tarnished silver-ware. A meal had obviously been in progress when something had interrupted; and the shriveled remains were indeed of breakfast.

Timothy scanned the mummified fare. "I believe that is called Full English."

"Wish it still was," said Randy. "Now it's like all-you-can-eat for ghosts. ...'Least there's not a bunch of skeletons sittin' around this table."

"Such a hearty breakfast," said Thomas, "would seem to rule out sickness or plague as reasons for abandoning ship."

"There may still be sustenance here for the living," said Tiya, tak-ing the lantern from Donte and padding into the galley.

"After all this time?" said Randy.

"There is tinned food in the larder," called Tiya. "Bully beef, sardines, deviled ham, various fruits and vegetables. And coffee, tea, and cocoa in tins."

"But, it's a hundred years old."

Timothy said, "Tinned food was found on a riverboat that sank in the 1860s, and was perfectly edible, though lacking a little in flavor."

"Assuming," added Thomas, "tinned food from the 1860s ever had much to begin with."

"And three-thousand-year-old honey," said Donte, "found in Egyptian tombs, was also still perfectly edible."

"Oh," said Randy. "Guess you know about puffy cans? My mom told me that."

"There are several," called Tiya. "But I may produce us a passable breakfast after we finish our search. The stove burns coal, and the bin is half full."

"We should have more light," said Donte. He reached up to shake one of the lamps. "There is still oil."

"Which," said Timothy, reaching up to shake the other, "would indicate it was daylight when the crew abandoned ship. If it had been early morning and dark... and since they seemingly left in haste... these lamps would have been left alight and burned up all their oil."

"The more we find," said Donte. "The more the mystery deepens." Taking match from a pocket, he opened the lamp and lit the wick. The flame was feeble and blue at first, but gradually grew to a golden glow and the darkness retreated to shadowy corners.

"What is strange," said Timothy, lighting the other lamp, "and that is a very relative term in light of what we have so far seen... is that the food on this table was not devoured by rats. Surely there would have been rats aboard?"

"I doubt they took their rats with them," said Thomas.

Randy asked, "You sayin' the rats abandoned her, too?"

"Or perhaps, there were none," said Donte.

Tiya returned from the galley. "It is said that rats will not embark aboard a ship they sense is doomed."

"I've read that," said Randy. "But I thought it meant rats wouldn't get on a ship that was gonna sink."

"She didn't sink," said Thomas. "To state the obvious."

"Were there rats on the *Titanic?*" asked Randy.

"I have not read there were," said Donte. "But, of course, she was new. And perhaps *Dorrit Foxley's* cargo was nothing rats could eat and that was the reason there weren't any." He took the lamp down from its hook. "Let us continue our search."

Tiya smiled. "You are eager to see the engine room."

"It does not take a *Mambo* to perceive that. But, first every space on this level, and then the crew quarters below."

"Then breakfast?" asked Randy. "Assumin' there's no one aboard but us."

"*Wi*," said Tiya. "Since, it would seem, no spirits remain... except, perhaps, *her* lonely soul... I am eager to challenge my cooking skills with what sustained mortal forms in the past."

FOURTEEN
Katòz

"The crew quarters," Donte observed, after leading down a companionway to the open door of a large com-partment, its nether darkness defying his lamp, and echoes awakening as he spoke.

They had searched the upper levels -- the captain's, mate's, and engineer's cabins, the cook's adjacent to the galley -- and though finding many interesting things, they were, as Donte reminded, when tempted by the engineer's collection of technical books, looking for signs of recent life.

He stepped though the doorway...

Something pale and shapeless flew at him out of the dark!

Dodging back, almost dropping the lamp, Donte swung his bar one-handed, hitting something soft and *pulpy*, and there was a fleshy-sounding thud.

Randy charged in past him, swinging his bar with both hands. "Fuck you!" he yelled, beating at something soft and white that now seemed to writhe on the deck.

Donte raised his lantern as Randy struck the thing again. There was another fleshy thud, and it seemed to go still.

Tiya, with one of galley lamps, her own bar ready in hand, came in and looked at what lay at their feet. "You two have killed a sea bag."

"But it *jumped* at Donte! I *saw* it!" puffed Randy. He poked the white canvas bag with his bar, then warily nudged it with a toe.

"*Non*," said Donte. "It simply fell from this upper berth." He gripped Randy's shoulder. "But I am glad you are at my back."

90

Timothy entered, and Thomas followed with the third lamp. Timothy regarded the bag. "After lying up there a hundred years, it chose this moment to fall."

Cautiously parting the privacy curtains, Tiya looked into the berth. "There is no one to have pushed it, alive or otherwise."

Donte gazed around the bunk-lined compartment: down here, as in the cabins above, less exposed to the elements, all was far better preserved; there was no mold or extensive decay, and the white paint was mostly intact, which made the glow of the lamps much brighter. Besides her engineer, mate, cook, and captain, *Dorrit* had been crewed by eight, two of them probably seamen, two serving as oilers and wipers, and the others stokers to fire her boiler. As in the cabins they had searched, here also were signs of a frantic departure: lockers rummaged and open, clothing lying strewn about, and sea-bags only party packed, including the one they had beaten.

"Looks like they just left," panted Randy, brushing his hair out of his eyes. "That's kinda spooky woo woo, too."

"What is most strange," said Timothy, "is though whatever threatened them apparently happened suddenly, they thought at least they had enough time to pack their personal things."

"*Wi*," said Tiya. "But then whatever they feared became so compelling or intense they left it all behind."

"World War One!" exclaimed Donte. "Begun in July of 1914, and ending November of 1918. This was a British ship, and Germany was their enemy. And it was 1916, the middle of that war. Germany had U-boats which torpedoed British ships, but it was common practice then... before the war became so savage... to allow a ship's crew to take to their lifeboats, then sink the ship with deck-gun fire."

"And more economical, saving expensive torpedoes," said Tiya. Then she shook her head. "So many resources wasted on wars and manufacturing things to kill."

Timothy said, "A seemingly logical explanation to this mystery. ...A calm, clear morning in June; the crew sitting down to breakfast. Then a U-boat surfaces. Her captain gives a warning, and *Dorrit Foxley's* crew run to get their possessions."

Donte nodded and continued, "The U-boat captain grows impatient because they are taking too long. Perhaps there is smoke on the horizon that might be an enemy warship. He warns he will fire in minutes."

"So, they all rush to their boat," said Thomas. "Leaving most of their things behind."

"But, obviously," said Randy, "the Germans didn't sink her."

"Perhaps they thought they did," said Donte. "She is a small ship; one shot would have sunk her if well-placed. But, perhaps it wasn't well-placed, and they left before confirming their kill?"

Timothy said, "The theory is sound up that point. But, since *Dorrit Foxley* was not sunk, why did her crew not return?"

"Perhaps a storm came up?" said Thomas. "And they lost sight of her."

"That, too, is sound... up to a point."

"The point," Donte finished, "of, where has she been all this time?"

"The Bermuda Triangle," said Randy. "Where spooky stuff supposedly happens."

"We will have time to ponder that after we finish our search," said Donte.

"I propose we ponder at breakfast," said Thomas.

Tiya examined another bunk. "The blankets and bedding are still quite good. Our people would be happy to have them."

"Here are old-school jeans," said Thomas, pulling a pair of dungarees from the beaten sea bag.

"They're a little long for me," said Randy, tucking them under his belly. "But they'll fit if I leave a few buttons open. ...But, ain't they dead guy's jeans?"

Tiya smiled. "I would say almost certainly after a hundred years."

"...Oh, yeah."

"And," Tiya went on, spreading her arms and turning around, "I feel nothing malevolent here; nothing to leave an evil taint on anything aboard."

Donte added, "A good lifeboat will survive most storms, and another ship may have rescued them, so it is very possible the former owner of those jeans lived, if not happily *ever* after, at least to a happy old age."

"I like the sound of that," said Randy, reaching to shed his loincloth.

"Shall I avert my eyes?" asked Tiya.

Timothy laughed. "You have already seen him altogether."

Randy laughed, too. "She might have missed somethin'."

"Boys!" huffed Tiya, and turned her back.

Thomas continued searching the bag. "Donte, he looks like you."

Everyone gathered around, Randy tugging the dungarees on, as
Thomas displayed a photograph of the type once known as a cabinet
card. Originally sepia-toned, it had faded and yellowed over the
years, but showed *Dorrit Foxley's* crew posed on her forward cargo
deck. The ship was docked in a port, and palm trees in the back-
ground ashore suggested the Caribbean.

"That could be Port-au-Prince," said Donte. "Perhaps when they
took on the rum. The United States occupied Haiti during World War
One to prevent any German incursion, and British ships would have
come there."

"They were integrated," said Randy, indicating the photograph,
"even way back then."

Timothy said, "Though, as did most so-called civilized people...
as many still do today... the British believed that darker races should
be denied the privilege of whites, they were a bit more enlightened
than the United States by that time."

"And," said Donte, "it was common to hire native sailors on ships
in foreign locales. And stokers... especially blacks... who could with-
stand the heat of engine rooms in climates such as this."

"You would have qualified," said Thomas.

"He surely did," said Tiya, indicating an ebony youth of maybe
fifteen years, muscular though padded with chub, who, like the other
native crew members, wore only dungarees. "He does resemble
Donte," she added, leaning close to the picture. "In face as well as
physique, though perhaps in a year or so." She touched Donte's
shoulder and smiled. "Which I look forward to seeing."

"He looks cool in the future," said Randy, then smiled and
touched Donte's arm. "'Course you look cool now."

The captain, engineer and mate, all of them Anglo-Saxon -- the former boasting a bushy gray beard, stout, and possibly in his mid-fifties, clad in cap and uniform coat -- stood upon one of the hatch covers, their crew ranked below them on deck.

Thomas asked, "Did another crewman take the picture?"

Timothy looked at the back of the photo. "It was taken by a professional, as many photographs were in those times. And it *was* in Port-au-Prince, and in 1916. Perhaps for advertising, so many copies would have been made."

"*He* musta been the cook," said Randy, indicating a fat black man in a white hat and apron. "They all look happy, I'd say. An' kinda like a family."

Donte studied the dim images: the captain did look genial, as did the mate and engineer; the former also in cap and coat, lean and aquiline-nosed, the latter a generously swag-bellied man in dungarees and chambray shirt. And their crew looked cheerful, though dark faces hadn't photographed as well as lighter complexions: and though the cook was grinning, and most of the others seemed to smile, the midnight youth who resembled him -- or how he might look in a year or so -- may have been simply showing his teeth in a natural parted-lips pout like his own.

"A good ship is like a family," he said. "And I hope, whatever happened to them, they all came though it alive."

FIFTEEN
Kenz

Tiya gave Donte a smile. "The time you have been eager for."

"I confess," said Donte, as, after descending another companion into deeper darkness, their shadows grotesque in the shifting lamplight, they stood at the engine room's watertight door. It was a quick-acting type, and, giving his lantern to Timothy, Donte grasped its iron wheel.

"It will not turn," he puffed, after straining a moment.

"Is it rusted?" asked Randy.

"Not very badly."

"Let me help."

"Counter-clockwise," said Donte, as Randy stepped to his side and both took a grip on the wheel.

"It moved a little," puffed Randy.

"Let us try in the other direction."

Again they strained, and the wheel turned a bit, and this time there was an iron clunk.

Donte said, "It seems to be jammed on the other side."

Timothy asked, "Could it be locked?"

"Such doors cannot be locked," said Donte. "At least they are not intended to be. Let us try again, and this time turn it back and forth."

Once more he and Randy strained on the wheel, and again there was an iron clunk as it turned a little but no more.

Timothy suggested, "Perhaps with one of our bars for leverage? And using my mass instead of your muscles?"

Randy laughed. "Donte's got the muscles, not me."

"Your strength is in courage," said Donte.

"Aw, it was only a sea bag."

"You did not know that," said Tiya, "when you leapt in to defend him."

"We all have our strengths," said Timothy "And fat may be mine in this case."

Donte inserted his bar into the wheel's spokes, and Timothy applied his weight, but the wheel remained immovable.

"Perhaps two bars?" said Thomas. "And my added fat."

"Three bars an' my fat?" proposed Randy.

"That would probably break it," said Donte. He tried it again with his hands. "I would say the wheel on the other side has been jammed with something."

"You sayin' someone could be in there?" said Randy. "...Like, maybe they ran in there to hide when they heard us comin'?"

"...Possibly," said Donte. "Though something falling against the door could have jammed the inside wheel."

Tiya called, "We mean you no harm!" in English, French and Kreyol.

Then Randy called in Spanish, but there was only silence except for occasional echoing creaks as the ship slowly rolled on the long gentle swells.

"A pity we know no German," said Thomas.

Timothy shrugged. "Or a thousand other tongues from Arabic to Zhuang. If someone is hiding in there... perhaps, as you said, who fears we are pirates... and cannot understand us, how can we reassure them? And we cannot claim salvage rights. Nor can we take anything, for then we *would* be pirates."

"But, where were they living?" mused Donte. "Even I would not live in the engine room... even if not an impractical place for someone guarding this ship. We have searched most of the logical spaces and found no sign of recent life. The forepeak is inaccessible; the cargo holds are battened; and no one would stay in the coal bunker."

Randy asked, "What about that high part in the stern?"

"The lazarette," said Donte. "Like the forepeak, used for stowage, often for paint and flammables... lubricating oil for the engine, kerosene for the lamps. It does seem the only probable place where we have not searched."

Randy examined the door. "Could you take out these bolts in the hinges?"

"The door is held fast by six dogs," said Donte. "Levers on the other side, which are engaged by the wheels. Removing the hinge bolts will not release them."

"There is no other way to get in?" asked Thomas.

"…Possibly though the coal bunker," said Donte, "though that would require a lot of digging since *Dorrit* was on a lengthy voyage and probably fully coaled."

"What about down the smoke stack?" asked Randy.

"The funnel draws out of the boiler's firebox; perhaps a possible access, but a difficult and dirty one." Donte considered. "There are ventilators to bring air down to the engine room; another possible entry. But for now we should search the lazarette. And, assuming we find no one alive, and if Tiya is still feeling challenged, perhaps a centuried breakfast?"

"I accept," said Tiya.

"Should we jam the door from this side?" asked Randy. "Stick one of our bars in the wheel in case there is somebody in there?"

"Imprisonment," said Tiya, "would not demonstrate we are friendly."

"Can you feel anything?" asked Donte.

Tiya pressed her cheek to the door. "It is harder to sense the living, especially what they feel or fear, than spirits of the dead." She was quiet a moment, the only sounds the creaks of the ship, then said, "I feel only loneliness."

SIXTEEN
Sèz

"**T**his is good," said Randy, "for bein' a hundred years old."

"Thank you," Tiya replied, laying a hand on Randy's shoulder as she placed a platter of fried bully beef amongst other fare on the table... deviled ham and kippered herrings, along with bowls of fruit from tins. There were also ship's biscuits from tins, palatable though hard and dry. They had brought their water cask aboard, and she had boiled a pot of coffee.

After leaving the engine room door, they had ascended to the main deck and gone aft to check the lazarette, passing the battened coal bunker and the two after cargo hatches -- which Donte confirmed were also secured -- to find the lazarette door rusted shut. By then a clear dawn was dispelling the stars, and a westerly breeze stirring the sea. Now, the galley was cheerfully lighted by sun streaming in through its open doors and pale salt-crusted portholes.

"Of course," said Timothy, forking kippers, "and as Benjamin Franklin said, 'hunger is the best pickle.'"

"I like pickles," said Randy, around a mouthful of kippers.

"Pickle also meant sauce in those times." Tiya seated herself between Randy and Donte and added some beef to her plate. "But there are actual pickles in jars. And tins of sugar, and honey. And, except for a few puffy cans, at least a month of food for many."

Randy laughed. "Lucky there was a can-opener."

"Ironically," said Thomas, forking bully beef, "tinned food was invented in 1810, but openers were not devised until 1856."

"So, how did people open 'em for forty-six years before?"

"Usually with a hammer and chisel."

Timothy turned to Donte. "What of water for you and Randy?"

"We will keep half of the longboat's cask," said Donte, around a mouthful of ham. "And there may be rain, which we can capture in buckets and pots."

Timothy sampled the ham. "A pity there are no eggs. ...If the wind holds out of the west, we should be home by this evening, and pos-sibly back by tomorrow at dusk. And, if we meet our fishing boat, they might be here this afternoon."

Tiya turned to Donte. "You do not fear *Dorrit* may sink?"

Donte sipped from his coffee mug after adding a spoonful of honey. "She still rides no lower than when we first found her, so does not seem to be leaking. Barring a sizable storm, I think she will yet live awhile."

Timothy spooned some mixed fruit. "The engine room concerns me... the chance of someone hiding down there. With the five of us on board he may be afraid to confront us, but, with only the two of you, and at least one at a time you must sleep."

"We will clean the sea-cabin," said Donte. "Open the portholes and wheelhouse windows and bring bedding from the crew quarters. Then one may sleep while the other stands watch."

"Still," said Timothy, "there would be only the two of you against a possibly full-grown man who may not speak your language."

"Or may not believe you," said Tiya. "As when we called we meant no harm."

"I will stay with them," said Thomas.

"Your courage is not in question," said Donte. "But your strength might not suffice should there be a hostile encounter."

"I will stay with you," said Tiya.

Timothy considered. "I would feel much easier if we could search the engine room before we left you aboard. ...You said there are ventilators?"

"Two of them," said Donte. "Those intake horns that flank the funnel, with shafts that go below. I should be able to climb down a line, but there are probably screens which would have to be removed."

"And no doubt badly rusted, and would take time to remove." Timothy studied the sparkling sea beyond a sunlit doorway. "This wind may not last through the day, so we should get underway soon." He turned to Tiya. "You would stay?"

"Most willingly," she replied, her arms encompassing Donte and Randy. "And there yet may be spirits aboard to challenge my *Voodou* skills."

SEVENTEEN
Disèt

"**B**on voyage!" called Randy, standing at the ship's bulwarks as the longboat's sail caught the wind, Thomas coiling the bow line and Timothy at the tiller.

"And stars to steer by!" called Donte, he and Tiya flanking Randy.

Now in full daylight, *Dorrit Foxley* was a forlorn sight, a rusty, corroded corpse of ship that seemingly should have sunk long ago, which saddened Donte as he turned away from the sparkling sea. "If this wind holds steady, they should be home by evening."

Randy waved a last time to Thomas, then also turned away, as did Tiya. "Will we still be here when they come back? In this position, I mean?"

"The morning wind prevails from the west, which is now moving us toward our island, and though it may shift to out of the east later this afternoon, that should return us to this position, or nearly enough to be easily found." Donte scanned around the horizon. "I see no other vessels, though some may pass today or tonight. At dusk we will hoist the masthead lamps, but for day we should fly a flag... perhaps there are some in the flag locker that have not decomposed. A Haitian flag, if there is one, and a breakdown signal... called a Blue Mike... to warn other ships we are not underway. But first we should access the engine room to ascertain that no one else is aboard. It would make no sense to examine the cargo or begin to gather things that may not be rightfully ours."

"But," said Tiya, "if you descend a ventilator you might find yourself with a frightened man who may not understand you."

"I think I can climb *down* a line," said Randy, flexing an arm that drooped underneath instead of bulging above. "So you won't be alone."

Donte smiled. "Thank you, *mwen fré*... in Kreyol, my brother."

"I like the sound of that," said Randy. "...An' I should get out of the sun. Guess they didn't have sun-screen a hundred years ago."

"I will make a potion," said Tiya. "There are medical supplies in the galley, which should include zinc oxide and petroleum jelly."

Except for the whisper of wind through the rigging and the gentle lapping of waves along the ship's massively-barnacled hull, there was only sunlit silence. ...But then, from below, came a faint iron clatter.

"What was that?" said Randy.

Donte signaled for silence; and again there were only soft sea sounds and an occasional rustle as wind ruffled tatters of hatch cover canvas. After a minute he said, "Something may have fallen. She is rolling more as the swells increase."

"Or," said Randy, "maybe somebody opened the engine room door!"

Donte took the capstan bar he'd leaned against the bulwarks. Randy and Tiya recovered theirs and followed Donte aft. There was a cry overhead, and they watched as a flock of gulls soared past maybe fifty meters above.

"They do not pause or circle," said Donte.

"Does that mean somethin'?" asked Randy.

"Gulls will often circle a ship in hope of something thrown overboard, such as scraps of food."

"And they may land to rest," added Tiya. "But, seemingly none have done so for a century."

A few minutes later, their lamps re-lit, they descended to the engine room door, where the echoing creaks of the ancient hull were louder and more frequent now as *Dorrit* rolled on the rising swells. Giving his lantern to Randy, Donte grasped the wheel. "It turns!"

"Has someone opened the door?" asked Tiya.

"I cannot tell."

Randy set the lamps on deck and raised his bar with both hands.

"We got your back, *mwen fré.*"

"*Wi*," said Tiya, her own bar ready.

Donte rotated the wheel, and there were squeals as the dogs released. With a glance at the others poised at his back, he pulled the door, hinges screaming, open. Another dank breath sighed out in his face, scented of rust, old oil, soot and coal. Recovering his lantern, he held it up and peered into blackness. The doorway gave onto a grating above a vast dark space below that echoed and eerily magnified the creaks and groans of the ship; and there were steep steps leading down. The glow of the lamp didn't penetrate far, but as his eyes began to adjust, he made out a trio of huge cylinders of a triple-expansion engine. Then he stepped over the doorway's high sill and lowered the lamp to look down at the grating. At his feet lay the mangled remains of the watertight door's inside wheel, two of its four spokes broken and its rim savagely twisted. Crouching, he examined it.

"Something of great force did this... a mighty sledge-hammer blow perhaps. And the shaft was almost sheared off. This is why the door was jammed, and the sound we heard up on deck was it falling."

Randy leaned over his shoulder. "But why did it fall off now?"

"Perhaps we broke what was left of the shaft when trying to force the outside wheel."

"But somebody musta done that," said Randy. "Like, maybe they hit that wheel with a hammer to jam the door so we couldn't get in?"

Donte picked up the broken wheel. "This damage was done many years ago, as evidenced by the rust... and I would not wish to confront anyone who could strike a blow such as this!"

"But," said Tiya, joining Randy, "if the crew abandoned ship, why was this door closed at all? Could not someone have run down here after we came aboard last night and somehow managed to dog the door despite the damaged wheel?"

"An' now they coulda got out!" said Randy, shooting a glance over a shoulder. "An' the wheel fell off when they closed the door so it wouldn't look like somebody *was* here."

Donte continued to study the wheel, turning it over in his hands.

"Such a terrible force! And obviously from only one blow." Then he looked up at Randy and Tiya. "It is normal procedure to close such doors when a ship may be in danger, such as during a storm... or if under attack in war, as we have surmised may have happened. But, as we found when we opened the door, the hinges cry out loudly, and that we did not hear."

Tiya said, "Perhaps it was opened stealthily?"

"...Perhaps," said Donte. "We will have to search everywhere again after exploring down here." Laying the wheel back on the grating and taking up his bar, he started down the stairway, Tiya and Randy following.

"The engineer's work bench!" Donte exclaimed, reaching the bottom of the steps and eagerly scanning the many old tools neatly racked above it, except for a hatchet, which lay on the bench among a scatter of wood chips. "All rusted, but not badly so, needing only some cleaning and oil. And what a big vise! I have always wanted a vise such as this!"

Tiya smiled. "You have only small vices."

Randy laughed, awakening echoes within the huge space. "Don't cream your jeans."

Tiya laughed, too. "He looks like he might."

Randy indicated the hatchet. "Looks like somebody was choppin' somethin'."

"Possibly a stopper for a leaking boiler tube," said Donte. He tested the hatchet's sharpness with a fingertip. "These are good tools and would be very useful... which is more reason to ascertain that only we are aboard."

He led the way to the boiler, its three fire doors all closed, and a shovel thrust into a fan of coal that spilled from an open bunker scuttle. "The fire was banked," he observed. "Which would fit our theory that the crew first thought they had more time to abandon ship."

"Why's that?" asked Randy.

"The engine was simply stopped," said Donte, "as the telegraph showed last night. Which could have been when a U-boat surfaced and ordered *Dorrit Foxley* to stop. The fire was banked by closing these doors, and the steam was left to blow off... there is a pipe on the funnel... just as I do with our tractor." He indicated the shovel standing upright in the coal. "It was not dropped in haste, which could mean the engine room crew was called up on deck but not told why. Perhaps so there would not be panic."

Tiya spread her arms. "The loneliness is strong down here... I feel it emanates from here; perhaps because this is the heart of the ship, once warm and throbbing but now cold and dead."

Randy regarded the fan of coal, chest-high where it spilled from the scuttle, and glistening dully like uncut black diamonds. "Musta been a lonely job, down here with nothin' but lamps an' the fire."

"And lonelier still," said Tiya, "for someone probably accustomed to living in sunlight and fresh open air. ...As, perhaps, was that boy in the picture."

"Which, as I said, is why," said Donte, "despite my love of mechanical things, even I would not choose to live down here. Though, because of the door being jammed, we had better ascertain that no one has been."

"YOW!" cried Randy. *"Look!"*

On the other side of the spill of coal, huddled in a sitting position, its back to the bunker's bulkhead, one hand and forearm buried beneath the heap of ebony anthracite, was a skeleton clad in nothing but ancient dungarees.

Randy drew back against Donte. "Spooky woo woo, man! I'm gonna see *that* in my dreams!"

But, Tiya knelt at the skeleton's side and lifted her lamp to study it. "Why should you fear someone's earthly remains?"

"...Yeah, guess you're right," said Randy, stepping nearer and raising his lamp.

"What do you feel?" asked Donte.

Tiya set down her lamp and gently grasped the skeleton's hand. "Only lonliness... if it is his spirit I feel and not that of *Dorrit Foxley*."

"Could they have become as one?" asked Donte, kneeling at Tiya's side.

"Perhaps," said Tiya. "They have drifted together a long time."

"He looks kinda small," said Randy, kneeling with Donte and

Tiya, the glow of their lamps a small island of light within the echoing dark all around. "Like he was young, I mean."

"*Wi*," said Tiya, gently laying the bony hand back on the skeleton's denim-clad thigh. "And, from the shape of his skull, his ancestry is obvious."

"...Yeah. Like it would fit in Donte's head."

"*That* is spooky woo woo," said Donte.

"Think he could be that boy in the picture? ...Or was, I mean?"

"I think it quite likely," said Tiya. "There have certainly been signs, which as I interpret them now, would not only seem to indicate that, but also that he has been calling to us and wanted us to find him."

"Signs?" asked Randy.

"It was his sea bag that fell from his bunk, and so we found the picture. And the wheel fell off the door, calling us down here and letting us enter."

Randy looked down at himself. "An' now I'm wearin' his jeans!"

"That is not spooky woo woo."

Donte touched Randy's shoulder. "Trust Tiya's judgment in spiritual things."

Tiya smiled. "As we trust yours in those of the sea."

Randy pointed. "Why did he bury his hand in the coal?"

"Perhaps the coal shifted," said Donte.

"Wonder how he died?"

Tiya inspected the skeleton and carefully uncovered the hand. "I see no injuries to his bones."

"I wonder..." said Donte. Taking his lamp, he returned to the stairs, ascended to the doorway, the door slowly creaking to and fro as *Dorrit Foxley* rolled, and pulled the door shriekingly shut. Then he picked up the twisted wheel and fitted it to the broken shaft as Randy puffed his way up the steps with Tiya following.

"What's up?" panted Randy.

Still holding the wheel in place, Donte studied the damage, then pointed to the hull plates on the ship's port side. "That would have been the trajectory, from just at *Dorrit's* waterline."

"The trajectory of what?" asked Tiya.

Laying the wheel down, Donte crossed the gratings to examine the hull.

"It's a big wooden plug," said Randy, joining Donte a moment later.

Donte nodded. "And the size of an 88 millimeter shell, as would have been fired by a German U-boat during World War One."

"But, that is small damage," said Tiya, coming to join the boys. "And was obviously sealed."

"Small," said Donte, "because the shell did not explode but only punctured the hull... see how the plate is bent inward around the point of impact?" He pointed back at the door. "Then it struck the wheel, making the door inoperable, then probably fell in the bilges."

"Like, it was a dud?" asked Randy.

"So it would seem," said Donte. "And that would fit our theory of what may have happened on a calm, clear morning a hundred years ago: a U-boat did fire upon *Dorrit*... a shot that should have sunk her, had the shell exploded. But it did not explode. And for some reason the U-boat... perhaps rushing off to attack other prey or sighting an enemy warship and diving in fear of being attacked... did not fire another."

Randy gazed into the darkness below. "An' he was still down here when the crew was abandoning ship, but the door was jammed an' he couldn't get out."

"Nor could the crew rescue him," said Donte, "because they were being fired upon and had to get away."

"He saved *Dorrit Foxley*," said Tiya. "By making that wooden plug."

"That is how it would seem," said Donte. "For she would have sunk within days had he not with water steadily pouring in."

"But, the crew didn't come back," said Randy.

"Perhaps, as Thomas suggested, a storm arose and they lost sight of her. And *Dorrit Foxley* drifted alone for a hundred years."

"But, you said there were ventilators," said Tiya. "Could not the boy have escaped that way?"

"Or couldn't he climb up the smoke stack?" asked Randy. "After the fire went out?"

Donte pointed upward. "The ventilators are too high to reach; nor could he have ascended the funnel without a line from above. And he was only a stoker... a 'native boy,' we assume, if he is the boy in the picture... and would not have known much about steam ships."

"But he had tools," said Randy. "Couldn't he have taken the door apart? Like, I'm sure you could."

"I have worked with tools all my life in the twenty-first century, but this happened a hundred years ago to a boy who was probably not familiar with mechanical things."

"Poor dude!" said Randy, again looking down. "So, I guess he starved to death?"

"He would have had water for several days... there is a cask for stokers... but there would have been nothing to eat. And, one by one, the lamps would have gone out, leaving him in darkness."

Tiya also looked down. "Poor boy."

"Are we gonna just leave him there?" asked Randy. "That don't seem right."

"We must try to find out who he was," said Tiya. "It is possible there are relations or family who should be notified. And he should be properly buried... perhaps on Little Orphan if we cannot identify him. But, though he has tried to speak to us, I cannot hear him directly. Or perhaps *Dorrit* is speaking for him."

"Perhaps there is something in his sea bag that would give us his name," said Donte. "Though, again, if he was a 'native boy...'"

"You mean black," said Randy.

"And in 1916, so he might not have had any documents."

Tiya asked, "Would he not have had to sign articles to serve aboard this ship?"

"Assuming he could write," said Donte. "If not, an X would have been sufficient."

"We should get a blanket," said Tiya. "And lay him to rest for now in his bunk."

"I say he deserves the captain's cabin for saving *Dorrit Foxley.*"

EIGHTEEN
Dizuit

"**A** pity we could not learn his name," said Tiya, about a half an hour later while following Donte and Randy back down the engine room stairs.

They had taken a blanket from the crew quarters, gently enshrouded the small skeleton and laid it to rest in the captain's bunk as if merely asleep.

Donte said, "It is not surprising he had no papers; and the captain apparently took the crew list when abandoning ship."

Randy asked, "Still think there coulda been somebody down here? I mean besides whoever he was?"

"Though it seems very doubtful, we should make absolutely sure." Donte strode around the engine room searching for signs of recent life -- blankets, food tins, empty rum bottles, but finding no such evidence -- while examining all the machinery and explaining many functions, first indicating the massive trio of vertical cast-iron cylin-ders, which ranged from a meter in diameter to twice, and then three times that size.

"It requires multiple expansions to get the most work out of steam, so here is a triple-expansion engine. From the boiler and through the throttle... that wheel up there above the foot-plate... steam enters the small high-pressure cylinder at 827 Kilopascals, or..." He turned to Randy. "...in Imperial measurement, about 120 pounds per square inch. This forces the piston down, which turns the engine's crank shaft, which rotates the ship's propeller. Then the steam exhausts to the second cylinder at greater volume but lower pressure... about 620 Kilopascals, or 90 PSI. The steam expands again, forcing the second piston down and further turning the crank shaft, then exhausts to the third cylinder at even greater volume but only about 206 kPa, or 30 PSI. There is one more expansion, and the third piston goes down, then steam exhausts to the condenser, turns back into water, and is returned to the boiler to repeat the cycle."

"How does the ship back up?" asked Randy.

Donte climbed to the foot-plate. "There is a Stephenson Link... this large lever... which operates the engine's valve gear. The engine is stopped by closing the throttle, the lever pulled back, then the engine is started again but turns in reverse and the ship goes astern. Of course there are many other controls, valves and things to adjust, as well as other machinery, such as the evaporator, which distills salt water from the sea into fresh water for the boiler."

"Why does it need fresh water?" asked Randy.

"Seawater when boiled leaves salt behind, which would clog the boiler tubes."

"Could you operate this engine?" asked Tiya.

"Yeah," said Randy. "Like, if you could get it started, we could take the whole ship home!"

"An intriguing idea," said Donte. "But I have only experience with our little steam tractor, and knowledge of larger engines only from books in our library. I do not know the specifics of how to operate this engine."

"But there are books," said Tiya, "in the engineer's cabin. Would they not have that knowledge?"

Donte glanced at the telegraph, which indicated FINISHED WITH ENGINE as he had left it last night. "This engine has not turned for a hundred years. And even if not rusted tight, the ship's screw is so crusted with barnacles it probably would not move."

"Could you give it full speed ahead?" asked Randy. "Like, to break it loose?"

"That could tear the engine off its bed. And, with her hull so fragile, could easily sink *Dorrit Foxley*." Donte climbed down. "It appears that, except for us, no one alive has been down here since the nameless boy died. But, we should search everywhere again, and, if possible, lock all the cabins."

"I saw a ring of keys in the captain's cabin," said Randy. "When we were layin' the poor dude to rest."

"Then we will go there first."

Tiya smiled as they passed the workbench to remount the steps, noting Donte's wistful face and laying a hand on his shoulder. "I do hope *Dorrit Foxley* is ours."

NINETEEN
Diznèf

R andy pleasurably patted his belly as he sprawled at the
galley table and muffled a surfeited burp. "That was awesome, Tiya!"

Tiya smiled. "Preparing hundred-year-old food is not a good example of my culinary skills... tinned beans, deviled ham, and tinned
fruit, along with some very aged spices."

Donte finished his beans-with-ham. "And awesome *Voodou.*"

"Say rather, good wishes upon the food that it nourish us in life."

Donte patted his own belly. "I often wonder if there would be
wars if everyone had enough to eat."

Randy fondled his fat again. "There probably wouldn't be wars if
everyone felt this good all the time."

It was early afternoon and the wind had diminished to barely a
breeze, the swells subsiding to slow-rolling humps on a softly sun-
sparkled turquoise sea. After leaving the engine room and closing
and dogging its door, they had searched all the officers' cabins again
and locked their doors with the keys. They had found a Haitian flag
in the wheelhouse locker, and a Blue Mike to warn other vessels that
Dorrit was not underway, and hoisted both up the foremast.

Tiya finished her bowl of fruit, took a sip of tea and turned to
Donte. "Are you now convinced we alone are aboard?"

"Almost."

Randy muffled another burp. "Thought we looked everywhere
twice."

Donte drank the last of his tea. "All the probable places in which
someone might hide, and which we have found accessible. Still, we

should wait before gathering things until either our fishing boat arrives... possibly later this afternoon... or Timothy returns tomorrow. We have to clean and air the sea-cabin, in which Tiya will sleep tonight, and bring new bedding up from below. We can place a mattress in the wheelhouse, so two may sleep while one stands watch."

"I should clean up the galley," said Tiya. "In preparation for supper, which may include Andre and Laurent."

"You should not be alone," said Donte, "until we are *absolutely* sure no one else is aboard."

He rose and went to the starboard doorway. "There are clouds on the western horizon, which may bring rain later today, so we should set out buckets and pots. Then we should fill a cask with water, stow some tinned food in a sea bag, and also unbatten a hatch cover in case we have to abandon ship."

"Still think she could sink?" asked Randy.

"After seeing the engine room bilges, I would say that only the barnacles are holding her hull plates together."

A few hours later found them all up in the sunlit wheelhouse. They had opened its salt-crusted windows, hooked back both of its doors, and also opened the sea-cabin's ports. Then they'd removed the moldy bedding and rotted remains of the captain's clothes, along with the sadly decomposed books, and thrown them overboard. Then they had scrubbed the woodwork and swabbed the floor with hot seawater and powdered galley soap, which banished the dank, musty smell. Tiya, assisted by Randy, had brought new bedding up from below, while Donte unbattened a forward hatch cover. Though too massive for him to open -- that would require a block-and-tackle rigged to the cargo mast -- it would now float free to serve as a raft if *Dorrit Foxley* sank.

He presently stood at the starboard bridge rail studying the still-distant clouds, while Tiya made up the sea-cabin's bunk and Randy arranged a mattress with a blanket and pillow on the wheelhouse floor. Despite the potion Tiya had made, and which she and Donte had applied to Randy's shoulders, chest and back, his paleness had shaded slightly to copper, which Donte remarked as he came out to join him.

"I used to be really tan," said Randy, "back in Malibu. Like I said we had a beach house an' I read a lot on the sun deck."

Tiya emerged and kissed Randy's cheek. "You will be even more handsome with a bit of color."

"*Notre beau garçon sauvage*," said Donte, also kissing Randy's cheek.

Randy smiled. "Boys kiss boys on your island?"

"When they are fond of each other."

"I like the sound of that." Randy kissed Donte and Tiya, then reached into a pocket. "I found these in the boy's sea bag when we were gettin' the mattress. Think they could still be okay?"

Donte regarded a packet of Players. "I would imagine somewhat dry, but let us find out." He pulled a match from his pocket.

Randy passed out cigarettes, and Donte struck the match on the rail. All took tentative puffs, then sighed out infant ghosts. They leaned on the rail, shoulder-to-shoulder, Randy in the middle, and smoked for a time in silence as wavelets lapped at *Dorrit's* hull and breeze strummed the rusty wire of her rigging. Then Randy aimed his cigarette west. "Are those rain clouds comin'?"

"Perhaps within an hour," said Donte, "if the wind does not shift."

"How do you learn stuff like that?"

"It is same," said Tiya, touching Randy's chest, "as learning the wisdom of your heart; you quiet yourself and listen, for everything in the world has a voice and is softly speaking to you."

"Guess I ain't been listenin'."

"Because you were distracted by things of no value shouting at you above the whispers of what really matters."

"A quiet place helps," said Donte. "As often found on a sea voyage."

"You mean to put things in perspective?" asked Randy. "Like, to learn what *really* matters?"

"You have already learned much," said Tiya.

Randy sighed smoke and gazed at the sea. "Guess my voyage started from where I had everything on a million-dollar yacht." He smiled and looked down at himself. "Now I'm in hundred-year-old jeans on a rusty old ship that could sink any time." His arms went around Donte and Tiya. "But, now I have friends, an' *that's* what matters."

"I believe the term is 'group hug,'" said Donte.

Casting their cigarettes into the sea, they all embraced for a minute. Tiya and Donte kissed Randy's cheeks, and he kissed theirs in return. Then he looked over Donte's shoulder. "There's a ship comin'."

Everyone turned toward the north, and Donte shaded his eyes with a hand. "A Disney cruise liner," he said. "They are painted in the old steamer style with black hull and white superstructure, as *Dorrit* probably was."

"She seems to be heading straight for us," said Tiya.

"They have probably seen us on radar, and will sight our Blue Mike and avoid us," said Donte.

Randy laughed. "Maybe the passengers will think we're part of their fantasy cruise? Like, 'look mommy, there's a ghost ship.'"

Donte laughed, too. "And we are the ghosts."

"So, where away, Captain?" asked Randy. "We got the sea-cabin an' wheelhouse clean, an' the buckets an' pots to catch the rain."

"Perhaps now," said Tiya, "with the two of you for protection... and a little assistance... I may tend to the galley? If our boats arrive today there will be hungry crewmen to feed and I will need clean utensils and dishes."

"We are at your command," said Donte. "Then we will get tools from the engine room and open the forepeak and lazarette doors. There should be oil for the lamps in the latter, and perhaps some gear in the former to raise the hatch covers and view the cargo."

"Guess it won't be treasure," said Randy.

"If useful to us it will be." Donte turned to descend the stairs, but Randy took his arm and pointed.

"That ship's still comin' straight at us!"

The rapidly oncoming liner, white water frothing a bone in her teeth, was seemingly on a collision course and showed no sign of veering away!

"Is the guy at the wheel asleep?" said Randy, staring at the approaching ship.

"Even if he were," said Donte, "which is very unlikely on such a luxurious ship, their radar would sound an alarm."

"But she is still coming at us!" said Tiya.

"Can't we do somethin'?" said Randy.

But Donte only stood at the rail watching the huge ship rushing at them, ten times the size of *little Dorrit*. "We have no siren to blow. No time to hoist another warning. And they seemingly have not seen the one we already fly."

"And apparently not even us!" said Tiya.

"But I can see people!" cried Randy.

Donte could see them, too; men, women, and children, almost all of them white, and mostly clad in swimming attire, many lounging in canvas chairs with drinks and plates of things to eat, families strolling the decks... and Mickey Mouse in a captain's cap waving from the bridge to cheering kids below.

"Prepare for collision!" yelled Donte. "Brace yourselves! Hang onto the rail! If we go down, swim away from the ship so she does not take us with her!"

He dashed into the wheelhouse, tore open several locker doors and found a massive flare gun. ...But, would it fire after all this time? Breaking it open, he jammed in a cartridge, ran out on the bridge, aimed at the sky, and pulled the rusty trigger. There was more of a WHUMP than a blast, but something shot skyward trailing sparks and exploded in a scarlet burst ahead of the oncoming liner.

But still the huge ship came on!

He threw his arms around Randy and Tiya. "Hang on!"

But then, in a minute, the liner rushed past, clearing *Dorrit Foxley's* flank by maybe ten meters at most, towering over *Dorrit* like an iceberg had dwarfed the *Titanic*. Donte caught a glimpse high above of a fat red-haired boy in swimming shorts staring down over the railing at them.

Then the huge ship was churning away, diesel smoke drifting back from her funnels emblazoned with famous mouse ears, and *Dorrit Foxley* plunging and rolling in the swirling froth of her wake.

"Fuck you, rodent!" yelled Randy, flipping a finger after the ship as she rapidly dwindled against the horizon. Then he turned to Donte. "Was that some kinda joke? Like, playin' ship chicken or somethin'?"

"That would be very unlikely," said Donte. "A captain could lose his license for doing such a dangerous thing."

Tiya asked, "But, how *could* they not have seen us? Even if not the helmsman, all those people on deck?"

"I think one did," said Donte. "A red-haired boy of maybe twelve."

"I saw him, too," said Randy. "For a second he looked like he saw a ghost."

Donte gazed after the liner. "That was also my impression from the shocked look on his face." Then he shrugged. "But, perhaps only coincidences compiling into a near-collision... a radar system malfunctioning; an inattentive watch; and parents with their children enchanted in their Disneyland."

"Like, makin' too much of their own noise?"

"...Perhaps," said Tiya, looking thoughtful.

"Well," said Randy. "Here comes the rain, an' I hope that don't miss us 'cause we need the water."

And it did not, for in minutes it swept upon them like a shimmering silvery curtain, drumming on the wheelhouse roof as they took shelter inside, and darkening the rusty decks of lonely *Dorrit Foxley*.

TWENTY
Ven

"I can take the watch now," offered Randy, shambling out of the wheelhouse, his low-slipping jeans mostly baring his bottom, their dragging cuffs puddled over his feet.

The night was hot and the air thickly humid from the recent rain, the sea glassy except for slow-rolling swells; and there were no sounds except the soft lapping of ripples around *Dorrit Foxley's* hull in an aura of pale luminescence. Donte, at the starboard bridge rail, regard-ed the Cheshire smile of moon now low on the western horizon. "It is yet an hour until midnight, do you not wish to rest any longer?"

Randy yawned and stretched, his jeans slipping even lower so only the spill of his belly in front kept them on his thighs. "Nah, ain't sleepy no more."

Donte glanced into the wheelhouse where the chart table lamp softly glowed. The sea-cabin's door was hooked partly open, and Tiya presumably asleep since no light shone from within. He kept his voice low not to wake her. "The engineer was very well-read besides his many technical books, and I brought a copy of *Kim* up here if you would like to read awhile."

"You went down there alone?" said Randy, also keeping his voice subdued. "What about stayin' together?"

"It is only a deck below, and all the cabin doors are locked so no one could be hiding in them. And you were here with Tiya."

"Guess you didn't see any ghosts?"

"*Non*, and the boy's remains are at rest. I lit a lamp for him."

"Guess he'd like that," said Randy, "after bein' down there in the

118

dark so long. An' if he was gonna haunt us I guess he woulda done it by now."

"Not all hauntings are spooky woo woo; and perhaps he already haunted us by calling us to find him."

"Or *Dorrit* called us to find him?"

"That is also possible."

"Wonder what other secrets she's keepin'?"

Donte gazed up at the funnel. "If *Dorrit* indeed has a spirit, she will reveal her secrets in time."

"Ever seen a ghost?"

"Once, perhaps a year ago. It was evening up on our mountain, and I saw a girl gazing out to sea."

"Think it coulda been her?" asked Randy. "The girl who loved the two boys? Tiya said her spirit still waited up there hopin' the banished boy's ship would come back."

"Perhaps it was," said Donte. "It is said that she watches over all who work upon the mountain: in the century that has passed there has never been another cave-in at the guano cliff."

Randy wobbled his way to the rail, the spheres of his chest rolling over the iron, his belly lolling out beneath, its pendulous weight deeply swaying his back as on the night Donte had met him, as he leaned beside Donte to gaze at the sea, a mirror of the star-studded sky so the ship seemed suspended between them. "I'll have plenty of time to read at home. ...I like the sound of that... at home."

"You may live with me if you wish: my father will certainly welcome you."

"I like the sound of that, too." Randy pulled out the Players pack and shook up two cigarettes. Donte struck a match, and both moved together to share the flame, then sighed out smoke and resumed their lean, shoulders touching, regarding the sea.

"No more close calls?" asked Randy.

Donte glanced to the mastheads, now crowned with lamps glowing gold. "Several vessels have passed while you slept; two freighters, another cruise ship, and a tanker, but none in close proximity."

"Guess Timothy an' Thomas didn't meet the fishin' boat."

"I have been watching the east and so far have not sighted her.

But, they should be home by now, and will probably return, along with the fishing boat, by tomorrow afternoon."

"An' we're still in about the same place?"

"We are probably closer to Little Orphan than we were last night, since today's wind was out of the west."

"Think she might drift there all by herself?"

"I suppose it is possible; though she would surely wreck on the reefs since we could not guide her into the cove."

"That would take a tugboat, huh? How close is someplace I could get to a phone?"

"Probably Môle-Saint-Nicolas, a town on Haiti's north coast, and the place where Columbus first landed in 1492. ...But then you would reveal yourself."

"I been thinkin' about that," said Randy. "You an' Tiya an' Thomas an' Timothy wanted me just like I was." He looked down at himself. "Just like I am, when you pulled me out of the ocean with nothin'."

"Which is how you came into this world, accessories not included."

"That *should* be what matters," said Randy. He flipped his cigarette toward the horizon. "But, what matters to the world out there *is* havin' all the accessories... which all comes down to money." He turned to Donte. "I don't wanna play Richie Rich, but I wanna do somethin' *useful*, like helpin' my friends when they need it."

Donte dropped his cigarette to perish with a soft sigh in the sea. "But, there *is* a world out there, and would it not try to reclaim you?"

"Trap me again," said Randy. "Like in some air-conditioned cage. Scream at me with its Disneyland noise until I can't hear those whispers that matter. An' lie to me like those kids on that ship... like Mickey Mouse is at the wheel an' everything's safe an' on the right course to some big magic kingdom." He pointed to the horizon. "But, *there* I have money an' I know how to use it. ...Your dad could be my guardian... legally, I mean... if he wanted to?"

"I have no doubt he would."

"I really like the sound of that." Randy kissed Donte's cheek, and Donte returned the kiss. Then hesitantly, or shyly, Randy slipped his arms around Donte and drew them together chest-to-chest, his lips meeting Donte's significantly. "I love you, Donte," he whispered.

For a moment Donte hesitated, but then gathered Randy all the more tightly and returned this much more meaningful kiss. "And I love you, Randy."

And for a time they stayed together, there on that forgotten ship adrift on the starlit sea.

But then Randy drew away and dropped his hands to his sides. "I need to tell you somethin'... like full disclosure, I guess."

"What is it?" asked Donte.

Randy took a breath. "When you were undoin' the hatch today, an' me an' Tiya were down below, in the crew quarters gettin' the beddin', me an' her... we kissed like that. ...Like you an' me just now."

"...Oh," said Donte.

Randy spread his hands. "It just sorta *happened*... it just felt right."

"...*Wi*," said Donte, after a moment. "One always feels when something is right."

"Like, when you an' me kissed just now?"

"That also felt right."

Randy gripped Donte's shoulders. "She loves you, Donte, she told me that. An' she's wanted to kiss you, like we just did, for a long time."

"...Oh," said Donte again. "That, too, I have wanted for a long time."

"She knows that," said Randy. "Maybe I shouldn't have..."

"Kissed her first?"

"If that was wrong, I'm sorry."

"I do not say it was wrong," said Donte. He touched a finger to Randy's lips. "And I feel you have shared that kiss with me."

"It felt like that," said Randy. "Like I was kissin' both of you... now *an'* then."

"It felt like that to me," said Tiya, emerging from the wheelhouse.

"Does that make sense?" asked Randy.

Donte thought for a moment, then said, "Why should it not."

"I love both of you," said Randy, as Tiya came to join them. He put a palm to his chest. "In here, for real, I can feel it. An' it don't feel wrong."

"And I love both of you," said Tiya, taking Donte and Randy's hands. "Which also does not feel wrong." She embraced Donte and kissed him now in the way he'd been dreaming she would.

Their kiss lasted long in the starlight, and Donte slipped an arm around Randy, drawing them into a triangle. "I love both of you, and that is not wrong."

TWENTY-ONE
Venteyen

"**B**reakfast, you two," announced Tiya, coming into the wheelhouse as the sun cleared the eastern horizon and burnished the breeze-ruffled sea.

Randy sat up beside Donte on the mattress spread on the floor. "I like the sound of that," he yawned.

"As do I," said Donte, also with a yawn. "...But, you were down in the galley alone."

Tiya knelt to kiss both boys. "I do not lightly defy captain's orders, but I do not feel any threat. And, since I had the last watch after Randy, I was already awake."

Donte rose and offered a hand to Randy, helping him to his feet. "You saw nothing of note while on watch?"

Tiya tugged up Randy's jeans, then gently smoothed Donte's hair. "Only a container ship on the southern horizon... though I suspect there *are* rats aboard because something made off with the bully beef leftover from supper last night."

"Guess it wasn't a ghost," said Randy. "Or the boy's skeleton got hungry."

"That I doubt."

Randy stretched and yawned again. "How could there be any rats now if there wasn't any for all those years?"

"Possibly drifting at sea," said Donte. "On a tree limb or other flotsam perhaps washed away in a storm. Or thrown overboard in refuse off another ship. Then sighting *Dorrit* and swimming to her. A rat could climb her rusty plates."

"Well, come, you two," said Tiya, "before it makes off with our

123

breakfast."

"Is that another ship?" asked Randy, pointing east as they emerged onto the port-side bridge.

Donte mounted the rail and looked eastward, shading his eyes from the sun. "I think it is Little Orphan... we must have drifted more last night. And the wind is again from the west, which will carry us closer."

"What if we keep on driftin'?" said Randy. "An' she hits the reefs?"

"Which would be sadly ironic," said Tiya, "after surviving so long."

"No doubt she would quickly break up," said Donte. "Being so aged and fragile, and we would lose everything aboard."

"Could we drop her anchor?" asked Randy.

"...Possibly," said Donte. "Though here it is too deep. We would have to wait for shallower water if she keeps drifting east. I doubt the chain would hold in a storm, but might keep her off the reef in good weather long enough to salvage."

"Or get a tug," said Randy. "An' bring *Dorrit* home to the cove."

"You would still do that?" asked Tiya, "despite revealing yourself?"

Randy spread his arms. "I got nothin' to hide."

"What of the weather, Donte?" asked Tiya.

Donte went into the sea-cabin and returned with a look of concern. "The barometer is still falling, and there may be a storm by tonight."

"What can we do?" asked Randy.

"There is little we can do but hope *Dorrit Foxley* still possesses the spirit and strength to live. I will inspect the anchor and ascertain if it can be dropped; but for now we should have breakfast to refresh our spirits and strength."

"I like the sound of that anyway."

A few hours later found them on deck gathered at the forepeak door with heavy tools from the engine room. The westerly wind was rising, though the sea was still fairly calm and whitecaps had not yet appeared, but a line of gunmetal clouds now darkened the western horizon.

Donte had examined the anchor and decided it might be dropped, though the only way to be sure was to do it... which could only be done once since there was no steam to power the capstan and raise the chain again. Then, after getting the tools, they had opened the lazarette door, finding two barrels of kerosene and three of lubricating oil among other supplies to maintain a ship, but no sign of anyone living there... though Donte, recalling what Randy had said up on the bridge the night before, wondered if *Dorrit* was keeping more secrets.

If she was, perhaps they were good ones; for a good feeling seem-ed to have wakened aboard, as if the ship was aware of them, and maybe even welcomed them. ...Or, perhaps this new feeling had come from themselves, awakening under silver starlight as they had embraced and kissed and proclaimed their newborn triangle of love.

Now, Donte, a huge wrench in hand, peered through the open porthole into the small triangular space. "Coils of line for docking, spools of wire for the rigging, bolts of canvas to cover the hatches, and extra blocks for the cargo booms."

Returning to the door, he fitted the wrench to one of its dogs and, with Randy and Tiya's help, forced it, screeching, to release. Then they released the other three and pried the door open with their bars, its rusted hinges screaming. Sunlight fanned in through the doorway, and Donte stepped over the sill.

Something moved in the shadows!

At first Donte thought of his own shadow... the sunlight at his back. He stopped... but something blacker than shadows seemed to move again!

"Somethin' wrong?" asked Randy, leaning in through the doorway.

The shadow lunged at Donte!

Donte leaped back, slamming into Randy, seeing a spear aimed at his heart!

There were shouted threats in a frightened voice... but in another language.

Randy and Tiya flanked Donte, their bars poised ready to strike, as Donte backed away from the door, the wooden spear still aimed at his chest and the voice, pitched high, shouting threats.

He realized he knew that language.

Spreading his arms to restrain his companions, he softly said in the same tongue, "Do not fear, we mean you no harm."

"It's a little kid!" exclaimed Randy, as the shadow framed itself in the doorway... an ebony boy of maybe eight, naked, and childishly sway-backed, his tummy roundly prominent, though his tight little chest and upper arms were solid with youthful muscle. His face was wide-nosed and cherub-cheeked, his eyes large and obsidian-bright, though fiercely narrowed now beneath a bushy cap of hair. The spear, Donte saw, was a swab handle, but sharpened to a deadly point.

For a moment the boy looked uncertain, then cursed and lunged at Randy.

Donte grabbed the spear and wrenched it out of the boy's small hands.

"He is our friend!" shouted Tiya, also in the boy's language, as he cowered back in the doorway and suddenly burst into tears. She stepped between Randy and Donte, and knelt to comfort the boy, saying soft things as she took his shoulders and gently drew him to her.

"What language is that?" asked Randy.

"Our own mother tongue," said Donte, examining the swab-handle spear, "though perhaps a different dialect."

"You know that, too?" asked Randy. "Besides English, French an' Kreyol?"

"We know it from history lessons, but seldom speak it out of school; though Tiya knows it much better than I because it is used in *Voodou*."

"Guess that explains why he didn't come out when we called all those times. ...What did he yell at me?"

"'You will not take me back,'" said Donte.

"...Take him back where?"

Tiya and the boy had been talking as his sobbing subsided. Now she turned to Randy and Donte. "To the slave ship."

TWENTY-TWO
Vennde

"**H**is name is Pereko," said Tiya, holding the little boy's hand as they walked aft to the galley. "He is very hungry and thirsty."

"Guess that's where the beef went," said Randy.

"*Wi*, he crept in and took it last night when we were up in the wheelhouse. But except for that, spearing a fish, and catching some rain in a piece of canvas, he has had nothing for a week."

"He has been aboard for a week?" asked Donte.

"Seven days, if I understand him."

Randy looked puzzled. "But he coulda busted a porthole an' gotten into the galley, since he's small enough to fit through."

"I do not understand all he says," said Tiya. "Much of his speech seems archaic... as you might speak eighteenth-century English... but he seems to know little of ships."

"But, what did he mean about a slave ship?"

"Sadly," said Donte, "they still exist. Haitian children are sometimes captured to work in the Dominican Republic."

"But, he can't be Haitian, can he? He doesn't speak French or Kreyol."

"For now he must eat," said Tiya. "There is plenty of time for questions later."

About an hour later, Tiya emerged from the sea-cabin, coming out on the port-side bridge where Randy and Donte stood at the rail.

"Pereko is asleep, exhausted from his ordeal. He was terrified of this ship, especially at night, and could hardly sleep at all. He spent his first two nights on deck, but finally worked up the courage to climb through the porthole into the forepeak and make a bed in the canvas. He found a rusty sailor's knife and carved the spear to fish."

"But, how did he get aboard?" asked Randy. "We had to climb up a line."

"Apparently there was a storm when he leapt overboard from the slave ship, and a wave swept him onto *Dorrit's* deck. He said he did not even see her until he found himself washed aboard: he had expected to die in the sea, preferring death to slavery."

"But, why did he hide from us?"

"He was watching us approach on the night we came aboard, but then saw you and feared we were slavers coming to recapture him."

"...Oh," said Randy. "I'm sorry."

Tiya lay a hand on his shoulder. "You have nothing to be sorry for."

"The past is not of your doing," said Donte, also touching Randy's shoulder. "And the future is ours to make."

"But, why was he scared of this ship? *Dorrit Foxley* saved his life."

"He has never seen a ship made of iron." Tiya gestured at the sky. "To him she is like a flying saucer from another world."

"An' we're like Little Grays?"

"No doubt we seemed very alien to him, not only knowing about this strange ship... which he assumed was ours... but also being together as equals." Tiya smiled. "He watched us on the bridge last night."

"Guess that is pretty alien, even on this world."

"Perhaps we can make that less so in our future."

"So, where could he be from? Like, some really primitive place?"

"I cannot imagine," said Tiya, "any place in the world today where ships of iron would be unknown. ...Or, for that matter, food in tins, which was also amazing to him. But he will probably tell us more after he has rested."

"We have other concerns," said Donte, scanning the sea, which was growing choppy, with whitecaps crowning some of the waves. "We are still drifting toward Little Orphan, and the wind is growing stronger. Did you observe the barometer, Tiya?"

"It is falling steadily; a storm, as you said, is coming."

"And we will be nearing the reefs by tonight."

"Sure you can't start the engine?" asked Randy.

Donte considered. "I suppose we could at least try, since there is nothing else we can do; though bringing such an engine to life requires much more than pushing a button. First we would have to fire the boiler... assuming there is make-up water still in the condenser... and it will take hours to build up steam. And if the engine has not seized, still the screw may not break free. Nor may the rudder, so we could not steer."

"Is it not worth trying?" asked Tiya.

"Yeah," said Randy. "If we can't do nothin' else to save her."

"You are right," said Donte. "We might yet bring *Dorrit Foxley* home."

"I like the sound of that."

Tiya pointed eastward. "There are sails."

"Our boats," said Donte, shading his eyes. "Tacking, of course, against the wind... but seemingly heading more to the south than directly toward us. ...But surely they have seen us."

"Should we shoot a flare?" asked Randy.

Donte continued to study the sails. "They *have* to have seen us by now, yet if they stay on their present course they will pass at least a kilometer south... *wi*, fire a flare."

Randy went into the wheelhouse, loaded and cocked the huge pistol, returned to the bridge, aimed the gun skyward and pulled the trigger. There was a pop, but nothing happened. "Damn, it's a dud."

He started to open the breech, but Donte yelled, *"NON!"* snatched it out of Randy's hands and flung it over the rail. Halfway to the sea it exploded in a scarlet burst. Everyone ducked and covered their faces as bits of fire and metal rained down.

"It was a hang-fire," said Donte. "The cartridges are so old."

"They *must* have seen that," said Tiya, looking toward the sails.

Donte studied the boats again. "It seems impossible they could not... yet they have not altered course."

Another voice spoke behind them, and Pereko, looking frightened again, appeared in the wheelhouse doorway.

"What did he say?" asked Randy.

"He thought it was a cannon," said Tiya. "The slave ship firing upon us and coming to take him back."

"Poor little dude," said Randy, slipping an arm around the boy. "Now what did he say?"

"He sees the sails," said Tiya. "I told him they are our friends. ...He asks why they are not coming to us."

"A significant question," said Donte. "I begin to think there is something here that requires your spiritual knowledge. No one on the Disney ship seemed to see us... except, perhaps, that red-haired boy. Nor, it seems, do the crews of our boats."

Randy's eyes widened beneath his blond mane. "You sayin' we really *are* ghosts?"

TWENTY-THREE
Venntwa

"**P**erhaps we will find out soon," said Donte. "The boats have tacked to the north again, and even if they cannot see us... for some as yet unexplainable reason... should be within hailing distance in less than half an hour."

"But, what if they can't hear us?" said Randy. "...An' if we *are* ghosts, when did we die?" Then he shivered under the sun. "Or, maybe only I died? When I jumped overboard from the yacht. Maybe you didn't see me? ...Like, maybe I'm back there drownin' right now, an' my mind is just makin' this up... you rescuin' me, findin' this ship, an' everything else that's happened?"

"I have read a book," said Donte, "with a very similar plot: a sailor in World War Two was blown overboard when his ship was torpedoed, but managed to swim to a tiny bleak island and spent many days there fighting to live. But in the end it was revealed that he had drowned in less than a minute after falling into the sea."

"An' his mind made the whole thing up?" asked Randy. "In the last seconds before he died?"

"I, too, have read *Pincher Martin*," said Tiya. "But, while I cannot yet explain what seems to have happened to us, I do not accept *that* explanation." She smiled and kissed Randy's cheek. "Though, if it were truly so, it touches my heart that you loved us."

"And mine," said Donte, also giving Randy a kiss; and Pereko smiled.

"Nor," added Tiya, "do I accept that we are all dead, which would be spooky woo woo."

"So, what you think's goin' on?" asked Randy. "How could this ship have been driftin' a hundred years an' nobody found her? ...An' why did we find her?"

"Perhaps she wanted us to find her."

Randy snapped his fingers. "The Bermuda Triangle! That's gotta be it! Like you said about things gettin' spirits. Maybe *Dorrit* got her spirit in there?" Randy turned to Donte. "Both of you said she felt lonely, so maybe she wanted a crew again? ...An' maybe that's why Pereko is here? He said a wave washed him onto her deck. What's the chance of that?"

"It is not unheard of," said Donte.

"You said a good crew is like a family." Randy looked at Pereko. "An' we're kinda like a family, so *Dorrit* wants to keep us forever."

"It will not be forever," said Donte. "If she continues drifting east she will die on the reefs by midnight."

Tiya said, "Perhaps she did want us to find her, but I do not think she can keep us aboard if we do not wish to stay."

Donte studied the boats again. "I might ascertain that: if they hold to their present tack they will pass within easy swimming distance if I set out now." He fingered the rusty rail. "Perhaps a distortion of time surrounds *Dorrit* and somehow she is not in the present? Perhaps, as Randy proposes, some of the Triangle still lingers around her... as a vessel sails out of a mist and brings a few ghosts of it with her. But, if I swim away from her, perhaps the others will see me."

"But, what if they don't?" said Randy. "An' what if you swim away from *Dorrit* an' *you* can't see her no more?"

"Randy is right," said Tiya. "We do not understand what has happened to us, and so we must be careful. If we are in a distortion of time, how far does it extend around us? Like the Bermuda Triangle, does it have a definable border, or does its phenomena gradually fade? If *Dorrit* is somehow still in the past, you might not be able to reach the present in time for those on the boats to see you; and you *could* lose sight of her."

"An' that's a long swim to the island," said Randy. "Think you could make it, Donte?"

"I would not wish to try."

"An' what if *Dorrit* is out of time... like, not synchronized or somethin'? Maybe she won't hit the reefs?"

"Time has still aged her," said Donte. "And she is still subject to natural forces... rust, barnacles, wind and sea; and rain still falls upon her. Perhaps our boats, like the cruise ship might have, would simply pass through her as if though a ghost because she is not there in their time."

"Like, they'd be goin' though where she *was* instead of where she is... or maybe where she isn't yet."

"But the reefs have been there for thousands of years and, unlike our boats or the Disney ship, they do not move, and have not moved."

"Which might explain why," said Tiya, "in all the time *Dorrit* has drifted, birds have never landed on her. Barnacles and seaweed grow, and of course she rusts, but those things happen in any time."

Randy asked, "But, how could Pereko spear a fish?"

"Only one in seven days," said Donte. "I would think him much more skilled."

"Like, maybe he just got lucky an' speared a place where a fish would be? ...Or maybe where a fish had been?"

"Or, to be spooky woo woo,'' said Tiya, "perhaps a fish that died at that moment."

Pereko had been listening, sensing the feelings behind the words if not comprehending the subject. He obviously knew something was wrong and turned to question Tiya.

"This will be difficult," said Tiya. "Trying to explain in his language what I cannot understand myself."

"Then perhaps that should wait," said Donte. "He has already suffered too many ordeals and should not be frightened any more."

Then he mounted the railing as the distant boats continued to near: they were still holding a northerly tack, heeling to the rising wind, spray flying up as their bows smacked the waves, which were growing larger and all capped in white, but no one aboard them seemed to have sighted the ship they would soon be passing. Timothy sat at the longboat's tiller, while Thomas stood scanning ahead in the bow. Andre captained the fishing boat, which followed some distance astern, with Laurent in her bow also scanning ahead. Donte cupped his hands to his mouth and leaned out over the sea as if that tiny additional distance might make any difference.

"AHOY! THOMAS!"

Tiya and Randy came to the rail, Pereko still nestled to Randy. Seconds passed... then maybe a minute... then Thomas cocked his head and looked toward them.

"AHOY! THOMAS!" called Donte again.

"OVER HERE!" yelled Randy.

Then Pereko called.

"What did he say?" asked Randy.

"Come to us," said Tiya.

"I think Thomas sees us!" cried Donte.

Thomas had mounted the longboat's gunwale, a hand on the mast to steady his bulk, the other shielding his eyes from spray as he gazed in *Dorrit's* direction. Then he turned to Timothy, called to him, and pointed.

"AHOY!" Donte shouted again, and everyone else joined in, Pereko also calling the word.

Timothy stood and looked toward the ship, also shielding his eyes. Then he shifted the tiller and shouted to the fishing boat, where Andre altered course to follow.

"What did you see?" asked Donte, as a short time later at the bulwarks on *Dorrit's* forward cargo deck, he caught the line heaved up by Thomas.

"At first, after hearing your hail," said Thomas, "which seemed to come out of nowhere, I only saw the faint ghost of a ship."

"*Wi*," said Timothy, lowering the sail. "Like a ship appearing out of a mist... but there is no mist."

A few minutes later, Donte, Randy, Pereko and Tiya had hoisted the other boys aboard.

"Who is this?" asked Timothy.

"His name is Pereko," said Tiya. "Beyond that we know little."

Pereko naturally approached Thomas, they being about the same age.

"What did he say?" asked Randy, catching the line heaved up by

Laurent as the fishing boat now came alongside, bucking upon the choppy waves slapping *Dorrit's* flank.

Thomas smiled. "He said we must live in wonderful place if children can become so fat."

Timothy asked, "Has he been guarding the salvage rights?"

"He was aboard," said Tiya, "seven days before we found her."

"Then, by maritime law she is his."

"Spoken like a chief," said Donte.

"I will add that," said Tiya, "to a list of many things I will be explaining to him... and some I have not yet explained to myself."

TWENTY-FOUR
Vennkat

"D o you think you can bring her to life?" asked Timothy, wobbling his way down the engine room stairs, both hands on the rails to steady his mass as *Dorrit* rolled on the still-rising waves.

The vast space was lighted by lamps and lanterns swinging to and fro, the temperature rising rapidly as Pereko and Randy, both gleaming with sweat -- Pereko now in a loincloth since there were no dungarees aboard small enough to fit him -- pitched coal into the firebox, their bodies reflecting the glare of flames as if they were imps sent to raise an inferno, while Tiya with an oil can was filling the engine's crank-bearing cups.

"The engine has not seized," said Donte, standing on the footplate, the engineer's technical book in hand, and watching a steam pressure gauge, its needle slowly climbing. "We ascertained that with the jacking bar... at least it moved a bit." He looked down at the massive propeller shaft tunneling aft beneath the deck plates. "But the question remains if the screw will turn. And even if so, will the rudder break free? We cannot save *Dorrit* unless we can steer."

Timothy, still gripping the rails as *Dorrit* rolled deeply to starboard, glanced at the tools on the workbench. "There are hammers and chisels. Andre and Laurent could take the longboat around to the stern and chip away the barnacles on the rudder gudgeons."

"That may help," said Donte. "But do you not need them to raise the hatch covers?"

"We have also been at work during the last few hours, and have already done that."

"You have seen the cargo?" asked Tiya, climbing out of the crank-pit.

"She carries coal aft," replied Timothy. "Probably from Jamaica, which, if we can bring her home, would fuel our stoves for many years and save the cutting of trees."

"And forward?" asked Donte.

"Ironically, guano in the foremost hold, which has been soaked with rainwater and is probably why she is down at the head."

"Guess you don't need that," puffed Randy, pausing to lean on his shovel and wipe the sweat from his black-dusted face.

"It would have increased our export but has gone rancid from being wet."

"What about the rum?"

Timothy smiled. "In the other forward hold." Then he turned to Donte. "But, the best for last: there are also trading goods... tools and axes, lanterns and lamps, dishes and cooking utensils... all well-crated and preserved. But, better still, and to your delight, there is a Hornsby tractor exactly like our own! It was wrapped in oiled canvas and still looks almost new."

Randy laughed. "Don't cream your jeans."

"Perhaps when he sees it," laughed Tiya.

Donte gripped the reversing lever as *Dorrit* rolled heavily to port, and Randy grabbed Pereko, who would have fallen against the boiler.

"That pleasure will have to wait," said Donte, as *Dorrit* recovered but then plunged to starboard. "We should rig a drogue from the spare canvas; that will bring her into the wind and stop this violent rolling, and also slow our drift."

"*Wi, mwen Captain,*" said Timothy. "Thomas and I will attend to that."

"I will not be captain, but engineer if we can raise power, so you will be in command."

"For now have you other orders?"

Donte held on to the lever again as *Dorrit* plunged into another deep roll. The groaning and creaks of her ancient hull were growing ominously loud as the mounting waves slammed and crashed against her, and from above came the keening of wind though her rigging and funnel stays. "The barometer?"

"Still falling, and clouds now cover the sky; the storm will soon be upon us." Timothy paused to listen. "It is beginning to rain."

"Secure the hatch covers again: we do not know if the pumps will work if she begins taking water. How far are we from our island?"

"Ten kilometers at most."

"Unless we *can* bring her back to life, she will wreck on the reefs by midnight... if the storm does not sink her first."

"What of the boy's remains?" asked Tiya, holding on to the footplate's rail as *Dorrit* rolled again, dropping deep in a trough between waves as if the sea was determined to take her.

"Still at rest in the captain's cabin. But we will bring him with us if we cannot save *Dorrit.*"

"We cannot keep the boats alongside" said Donte. "They would be battered to bits in the storm."

"We can hoist the longboat into the davits."

"Then we should send the fishing boat home."

"Would it not be safer to keep her nearby in case we have to abandon ship?"

"We need her to fish for our people, so she should not be risked. Nor should Andre and Laurent be asked to risk their lives."

"Now *you* are speaking like a chief."

"No doubt you would have thought of that. And we will have the longboat to hopefully save us if *Dorrit* goes down."

"There has been no time to load the boats with anything from her."

"Then we bring her home, or lose everything."

"Guess there's no time for dinner?" puffed Randy, pitching more coal in the fire.

Tiya smiled. "Another preparation if we are to battle a storm."

"Very true," said Timothy. "Strength for both body and spirit to face the fight ahead. But if you would help Thomas rig the drouge, I will attend to our nourishment, to which my strengths are much better suited."

"Then perhaps," said Donte, "a little *Voodou* to charm this engine?"

"That is your *Voodou* to do," said Tiya. "But, perhaps after rigging the drogue, Thomas will charm it with music." She stretched on tiptoes to kiss Donte's lips as he leaned down to kiss hers. Then she paused to kiss Randy while coming around the boiler.

Timothy cocked his head. "Has something new come aboard *Dorrit Foxley*... besides Pereko, of course?"

"Perhaps both new, yet timeless," said Donte. He checked the pressure gauge once more, then, consulting the book, went to adjust a valve on the boiler. "But there will be time to speak of that when we are home again."

"I like the sound of that," puffed Randy, pitching another scoop of coal into the hungry flames, his pendulous pillow of belly swinging freely to and fro as he turned back to the scuttle for yet another scoop.

Timothy smiled. "I am sure it will be enlightening, as will the story of Pereko." Then he turned around. "But now to face the nemesis."

"The storm?" puffed Randy.

"At present," sighed Timothy, "these stairs."

TWENTY-FIVE
Vennsenk

"The drogue has been rigged," said Donte, pausing with a wrench in hand while loosening a slider shoe on the low pressure cylinder rod. "*Dorrit* is coming into the wind."

"Yeah," panted Randy, zebra-striped with sweat and coal dust, his blond hair blackened and trailing lankly over his shoulders and chest, his sodden jeans clinging low on his hips as he paused to lean on his shovel. "She's stopped rollin' so bad."

The ship took on a long pitching motion as she slowly came around, her bow now cleaving the waves head-on, and the creaking and groans of her hull lessening.

"That will ease the strains upon her and slow our drift toward the reefs."

Pereko, also panting, spoke.

"What did he say?" asked Randy.

"It is not easy to translate, for he has no words for mechanical things, but he wonders why we are feeding this fire instead of trying to sail this ship away from the island reefs. Tiya explained enough for him to know the danger we face."

"Guess he don't know about needin' steam... but when *are* we gonna start tryin'?"

Donte went to look at the pressure gauge, then consulted the book again. "We are as ready as we will ever be."

Randy grinned. "Like, it's showtime."

Thomas appeared on the gratings above, his body gleaming with rain and spray. "Shall I play for *Dorrit?*"

"She will hear you as well in the wheelhouse," said Donte.

"I could help shovel coal."

"We all must do what we do best."

"Very well," said Thomas, then sighed. "Stairs!"

Taking the engineer's book, Donte went to a bank of valves, studied a page, then opened a valve. There was a hissing that carried above the crash of waves and keening of wind. "I have put steam to the steering engine: we must ascertain the rudder will move. If it will not, then all we have done cannot save *Dorrit Foxley.*"

He mounted to the foot-plate, opened the cap of the speaking-tube, blew into its whistle, then pressed an ear to the cone. A moment later Timothy's voice echoed metallically down, accompanied by the piping of Thomas.

"*Wi?*"

"Will she steer?" called Donte.

"I will try the wheel."

There was another hiss of steam, and from aft came grating squeals, along with chuffing sounds.

"Full turn!" called Timothy, after a minute as shudders and creaking sounded astern. "Do we also have engine power? It is now night and raining hard, and we are nearing the reefs!"

"A moment!" called Donte. He reached to the telegraph and moved the handle to STAND BY, its jangling bell awakening, then called into the tube again, "Have Thomas cut loose the drogue. When that is done, ring Ahead Slow."

"*Wi, mwen* Chief Engineer."

"Haul down the Blue Mike," Donte added. "And light the navigation lamps."

"If we cannot be seen, why light them?"

"Perhaps there are other ghost ships on the sea."

"Probably many," said Tiya, coming down the stairs. "Though perhaps *Dorrit* will yet live again."

Randy panted, "It would *really* be spooky woo woo if we got her home an' nobody could see us!"

"That remains to be seen," said Tiya. "Let me take your shovel; you have performed heroics enough." She patted Pereko's shoulder.

"As has he; and both of you should rest awhile."

"Perhaps you should not be down here," said Donte, poised to open the throttle wheel. *"Dorrit's* hull could break any moment and she would instantly sink."

"Then she will take us together," said Tiya.

"Yeah," said Randy, as *Dorrit* reared up to crest a wave and water crashed over her foredeck. "I think she brought us together. ...But, what about Pereko?"

"Tell him to go to the wheelhouse, Tiya, and he will be safe up there," said Donte.

But, Pereko shook his head when Tiya translated, then spoke:

"He wants to stay with us," said Tiya, as the boy took her and Randy's hands and turned to smile at Donte.

"We are his family now," said Tiya, as Pereko went on. "He knows somewhere in his heart that his mother and father are lost to him, and he can never return to his home."

"I know how that feels," said Randy.

The telegraph jangled again, AHEAD SLOW.

"Now we see if she will live." Donte, answered the telegraph, then gripped the throttle wheel, using both hands to turn it.

There was a hiss of steam into the high pressure cylinder. The engine juddered and creaked on its bed, its massive rods shifting a little with squeals, the propeller shaft groaning below.

Donte opened the throttle wider, the engine creaking louder and straining against its mounting bolts, its rods moving a few millimeters, as did the propeller shaft.

"C'mon, *Dorrit!"* yelled Randy. "Donte, can you give her more steam?"

"Too much and the engine will tear from its bed."

"We are turning broadside to the waves!" cried Tiya. "She may capsize!"

Donte cranked the throttle wheel down and released steam through the funnel pipe roaring into the night, then grabbed the reversing lever. "It is stuck! Help me!"

Randy, Pereko and Tiya scrambled up beside him, and together they pulled back the lever. Donte opened the throttle again.

Once more came a hissing of steam, and the engine shuddered and creaked as *Dorrit* plunged into a frightening roll, her iron bones crying in pain. The row of rods moved a few millimeters... then a centimeter... then two... also the propeller shaft... while from astern came cracking sounds as of rock being broken.

"Now ahead!" yelled Donte, again shutting down the throttle, releasing another roar of steam, then straining with the others to shift the lever forward. Then he re-opened the throttle, and again the engine shuddered and groaned, straining rods moving a little... then in seconds a little more... turning the propeller shaft to the rusty squeals of awakening iron and crumbling cracks of barnacle stone as *Dorrit's* screw broke free, the engine making a full revolution in a juddering series of jerks and jolts... then another still hesitantly... then a third more rapidly... then a fourth more smoothly and faster.

Donte screwed down the throttle a bit as the engine's revolutions increased and steadied into a slow-loping pulse at twenty-per-minute on the counter. The steering engine chuffed astern, and *Dorrit's* dangerous rolling lessened, transforming again into pitching and plunging as Timothy brought her back into the wind.

Pereko was watching the engine wide-eyed, and Randy put an arm around him. "Guess it's like a warp drive to him."

"As, once upon a time," said Donte, "it would have seemed to all of us."

The speaking-tube whistled.

"*Wi?*" called Donte into the cone.

"How much can we ask of her?" came Timothy's voice down the pipe, again accompanied by Thomas's flute. "We must claw away from the reefs, then set a course for the passage and arrive when the tide is highest at midnight."

"Ahead Half," said Donte, watching the slow-loping engine. "I would ask no more of her."

"That should be sufficient. The storm at least is getting no worse, and *Dorrit* with power is fighting it well. She was a good ship in her time."

"And still a good ship in ours."

Randy was listening, his cheek pressed to Donte's. "If we can get her back to it... or would that be ahead to it?"

"As Tiya said, that remains to be seen. But she is moving forward now and under her own steam; perhaps that will bring her back." Donte held the throttle wheel, warm and trembling to the pulse of the engine. "Perhaps, somehow and in her own way, she is alive again."

The telegraph jangled AHEAD HALF, and Donte opened the throttle wider, the engine's revolutions increasing to forty-per-minute. Donte confirmed the telegraph, then whistled the tube again.

"*Wi?*" called Timothy.

"How near were we to the reefs?"

"Perhaps you would not wish to know. Shall I send Thomas to help with stoking?"

Donte smiled at his companions, who looked very much like a family. ...Perhaps a family of the future. "We four are sufficient engine room crew with you and Thomas to guide *Dorrit* home."

TWENTY-SIX
Vennsis

"**S**he ain't rockin' an' rollin' so much," Randy panted, again pouring sweat as he shoveled coal, Tiya beside him also pitching, while Pereko sat resting nearby.

"*Wi*," said Donte, listening above the engine's pulse as *Dorrit's* motion grew easier. "Either the storm is passing, or we have come through the reefs."

"Perhaps both," said Tiya, with a hand to an ear. "The wind seems to be lessening, and the sound of waves breaking now comes from astern."

The telegraph jangled AHEAD SLOW.

Donte answered it. "We must be entering the cove."

The speaking-tube whistled and Thomas called down, "The storm is moving on to the east, and we are almost home. ...Timothy asks if we should beach her?"

"She deserves better," said Donte, "than to be beached like a derelict and left to fall apart on the shore. Bring her about like the good ship she is and we will drop her anchor."

"*Wi, mwen* Chief Engineer," replied Thomas.

Donte turned to Randy and Tiya. "We have sufficient steam, so rest."

"I like the sound of that!" panted Randy. He thrust his shovel upright in the coal, shook back his hair, which was now almost black, and patted his sweat-slicked belly. "Feels like I lost ten pounds."

"We will soon have all of you back again," said Tiya, leaning to kiss him.

"One of your breakfasts would be a good start."

"I hope I may do better at lunch with food of the present instead of the past." Tiya took his hand. "You have blisters."

"Ain't nothin'."

"You are one of the manliest boys I know, so there is no reason to act. And your hands are bleeding. Come with me to the galley so I may tend and bandage them."

"You cool here, Donte?" asked Randy.

"*Wi,*" said Donte, and smiled at Pereko, who'd come to look at Randy's hands and make a painful face. "He and I will drop the anchor."

The telegraph jangled ALL STOP, and Donte, replying, screwed down the throttle. For the first time in hours the rank of rods ceased rising and falling. Then the telegraph rang ASTERN SLOW, and Donte threw back the reversing lever, then replied and opened the throttle. Once more the engine came to life until another ring for ALL STOP. Then, after another moment, came the ring for FINISHED WITH ENGINE.

"Think she finally is?" called Randy from up on the gratings with Tiya.

Donte answered the telegraph, then stood for a moment gazing around within *Dorrit Foxley's* heart. "Perhaps that also remains to be seen."

TWENTY-SEVEN
Vennsèt

"**I** think they see us!" cried Randy, pointing to a trio of figures standing on the distant beach, their feet in the water lapping the sand, and seemingly waving to *Dorrit*.

It was now almost dawn, though the eastern sky was still curtained by clouds like a stage before a play began, and there was only silver starlight illuminating the glimmering cove, where *Dorrit Foxley* rested at anchor, smoke still ghosting faint from her funnel. The wind had diminished to barely a breeze trailing along behind the storm as a little brother tags after his elder, softly rustling the island trees and whispering through *Dorrit's* rigging, while gentle waves rippled along her hull with liquid musical sounds.

Though it might have been logical to lower the longboat and go ashore, they had gathered instead in the lamp-lit galley, where Thomas had boiled centuried coffee and Tiya had served an enormous breakfast approximating a Full-English as best she could with the present past food, sitting together at the table, while Pereko, his belly spherically stuffed, and comfortably lounging in Randy's lap, had told the story of his capture and weeks in chains aboard the slave ship until he'd managed to free himself and leap overboard in a storm. Timothy, Tiya and Donte had asked him many questions, but the answers in his archaic speech only left more mystery.

"It would seem from his description," Tiya had said when Pereko had finished, nestled to Randy and yawning like any young boy kept awake all night, "that he lived on the Ivory Coast, which was our own ancestral home."

"It would also seem," Donte had said in wonder, "the slave ship was a square-rigger of eighteenth-century design!"

Randy had asked, "Like the one you said got wrecked on your reefs three-hundred years ago?"

"From which our people... at least some of them... escaped their chains to begin a new life."

Randy had looked at Pereko, also with an expression of awe. "Could it have been the *same* ship? An' maybe he jumped overboard in the Bermuda Triangle, an' that's where... or maybe when... *Dorrit Foxley* saved him?"

Tiya had said, "Then perhaps she saved him twice, for many aboard the slave ship... and many of those were children... did not survive the wreck."

Timothy had concluded, "We may in time understand all this, but for now it would seem, wherever *Dorrit Foxley* has drifted, it was longer ago and farther away than our present minds can grasp."

Randy had asked, "What *about* the present? Like, where are we now? ...Or *when* are we now?"

Thomas had asked, "Should we sound the siren to wake the village? ...If there is a village."

"That would be rude," Timothy had replied. "Wherever we are... or maybe when... we seem to be in no danger, and, as Tiya assures us, alive in both body and spirit." He'd paused to pat his belly and politely smother a burp. "Which I certainly feel. We will go to the bridge and wait until daylight, when we will be seen... or not." Then he had turned to Donte. "Unless you advise another course?"

"Yours seems the most logical at present... whenever this present may be."

Now, up on the bridge with the rest of the crew, Donte mounted the rail to see better. "They are two boys and a girl... smiling, I think, and waving to us... but I cannot see them clearly." He leaned farther out, dangerously, and Randy's bandaged hands clasped his waist.

"I do not recognize them," said Donte, shading his eyes from the stars. "But, there is our fishing boat on the shore as Andre and Laurent would have left her."

"She is almost as old as *Dorrit*," Timothy said, also scanning the shore. "And we have always beached her there."

Randy said, "Guess that means, whenever we are, it's not more than a hundred years ago."

"A little less spooky woo woo," said Tiya, mounting the rail beside Donte and also shading her eyes.

"Perhaps they are visitors?" said Thomas. "Put into our cove because of the storm?"

"Then where is their boat?" said Timothy.

"Do you recognize them, Tiya?" asked Donte.

"*Non...* though I think they are older than us by perhaps a year or so."

"Or maybe a lot more years," said Randy, climbing up between Donte and Tiya.

"Perhaps you are right," said Tiya, still regarding the trio ashore.

"I don't think I wanna be right if it means what I think it does."

Tiya smiled. "A new life begins when and where it begins, and not always a time and place of our choosing; but I do think you may be right, though perhaps in another way."

"...Huh?"

"It is growing lighter," said Thomas. "We soon will be able to see them more clearly."

Tiya took Donte and Randy's hands, bringing them back on deck with her. "I think perhaps the opposite."

"Huh?" repeated Randy.

Tiya smiled again. "Other dimensions and warps of time, those I do not understand, but I know ghosts when I see them."

"...Oh," said Randy, after a moment. "But not who they are? ...Or who they were?"

"Regard them again and think for moment of what you have learned on this voyage."

Randy's eyes widened. "You sayin' it's *them*? Together now? Like they always shoulda been?"

"Would that be spooky woo woo?"

"No, it's cool."

"The banished boy?" asked Timothy, also regarding the trio.

"And the girl, and his friend?" asked Thomas.

"Why should it not be?" Tiya replied. "They have been waiting for him all this time."

Donte touched the rail. "And *Dorrit Foxley* was the ship."

Timothy said, "At least that much can be understood. The time was 1916, the year the boy was banished."

"To sign aboard as a stoker," said Donte, "on a trading steamer. ...*Dorrit* took on the guano *here*, then the coal in Jamaica, then the rum in Port-au-Prince and set off for Bermuda."

"An' we figured out," said Randy, "what happened after that. ...Or some of it, anyway."

"And now he came home," said Thomas. "Because we brought him... or *Dorrit* did."

"Perhaps she needed our help," said Tiya. "And that is why we found her."

"But," said Timothy, "she had already drifted close enough to wreck on our reefs if we hadn't found her."

Tiya pointed to the beach. "But then we would not have found *him*."

Randy gazed at the trio again, who now stood quietly holding hands as dawn slowly brightened the eastern sky. "They're gettin' harder to see."

"As are most ghosts in daylight," said Tiya. She slipped an arm around Pereko. "It would seem I have more explaining ahead."

"Guess they know what really happened, up on the mountain, I mean?" said Randy. "Back in 1916."

"I have no doubt they do."

"Then may I assume," said Timothy, "and to correct our records, the banished boy *was* telling the truth and did try to save his buried friend?"

Tiya waved to the figures, Pereko smiling and doing the same. "Speaking as your future *Mambo*, there is proof enough for me."

"Still, I wish, for our records, there was more tangible evidence than only the testimony of ghosts."

Donte laughed. "Spoken like our future chief."

"His hand!" exclaimed Randy, snapping his fingers. "*That's* why he buried it under the coal just before he died!"

"...*Wi*," said Donte. "To show he had not uncovered the hand of his buried friend."

"...*Wi*," said Timothy. "He knew he was dying and would not have lied. So his banishment is lifted, his good name and honor restored, and his earthly remains will rest with his friends." He turned to the trio and called, "Welcome home!"

The figures were growing indistinct as the sun raised its crown through the now distant clouds, but once more they waved, then turned hand-in-hand to walk along the brightening beach while slowly fading away.

"Hope we can do that," said Randy, taking Donte and Tiya's hands and forming a triangle around Pereko. "'Cept not the fading away."

"At least not for many years," said Donte.

Thomas was gazing around, an expression of wonderment on his face as dawn came to Little Orphan. "Look at *Dorrit!*"

The others also regarded the ship, and also with expressions of wonder. "She's new again!" cried Randy.

"For us she is," said Donte, seeing, as he had surmised yesterday, *Dorrit* in classic steamer colors of black hull and white upperworks, her funnel an ebony tower against the blue morning sky. "She is as she was in 1916 when setting out on a *very* long voyage, an even-then old but happy ship and home to her family of crew."

"*Wi*," agreed Timothy. "Not a galleon filled with gold, but still very much a treasure to us."

"Guess she's worth a lot now," said Randy. "Like to a museum or somethin'. ...I mean if we're back in the now."

Donte smiled. "You are still thinking of the world out there." He pointed toward the ocean horizon. "But your home is now here with us... whenever we are now... and *Dorrit* was a trading steamer, so why should she not be one again to the benefit of our people."

"Ahoy, *Dorrit Foxley!*"

"Andre and Laurent!" cried Thomas, as the fat and chubby boys ran puffing onto the shore.

Timothy said, "We are also home."

"And just in time," said Tiya, "for a second breakfast of much more timely ingredients."

151

Donte and Randy said together, "I like the sound of that."

FINI

ABOUT THE AUTHOR

Jess Mowry was born in 1960 near Starkville, Mississippi. When he was only a few months old his father took him to live in Oakland, California. Mowry's father was a voracious reader who introduced his son to books at a very early age. Jess attended a public school, but despite his love of reading, dropped out at age thirteen, part way through the eighth grade and worked with his father in the scrap-iron business. In his late teens, Jess moved to Arizona to work as a truck driver and heavy equipment operator. He also lived and worked in Alaska as an engineer aboard a tugboat and as an aircraft mechanic on Douglas C-47 cargo planes, as well as at a children's refuge in Haiti.

Mowry has written twenty-two books and many short stories about black children and teens in a variety of genres, ranging from inner-city settings to the forests of Haiti, the wilds of Alaska, the Arizona desert, the Caribbean Sea, and the African veldt. While some of his novels are set in Oakland and deal with social issues, such as poverty, violence, drugs, gangs, teenage sexuality, and school dropouts, Mowry has also written ghost tales, as well as novels featuring Voodoo and African magic, in addition to sea stories, and compiled an anthology of Victorian ghost stories.

Jess Mowry lives in Oakland, California.

THIS BOOK IS ALSO AVAILABLE IN A KINDLE EDITION

OTHER ANUBIS BOOKS

AVAILABLE ON AMAZON